THE BUTCHERS BOY

Lying In Wait At Aberlleiniog

K. E. Heaton

Other books from the same author:

Tales Of Entrapment – A Trilogy

Book 1 – Death On The Algarve: Eyes Of The Water

Book 2 – Uncle Joe's Revenge: Death On The Cut

Book 3 – Devoid Of Guilt: A Portuguese Harvest Of Death

Also by the same author:

She's Missing

Red Dust & Raindrops

The Italian Trap

**Text copyright © 2020 K. E. Heaton
All rights reserved**

This is a work of fiction. Names, characters, businesses, places, events and incidents are either the products of the author's imagination or used in a fictitious manner. Any resemblance to actual persons, living or dead, or actual events is purely coincidental.

No part of this publication may be reproduced, stored in a retrieval system, or transmitted in any form or by any means, without the prior permission in writing of the author.

The author appreciates your time and attention. Please consider leaving a review or telling your friends about this book, to help spread the word.

Thank you for your support.

K. E. HEATON

Dedication

For a special family with all my love.

Preface

Life on a Lancashire council estate was never easy.

And for a little boy like Robert Rudd, it was particularly hard.

He may have lived the first nine years of his life in the shadows of a dark satanic mill, but his future lay elsewhere.

The boy was just like his mother, ambitious and frustrated.

He was destined to follow in the footsteps of his namesake Robert of Rhuddlan "The butcher."

A tyrant, who in the eleventh century, ruled the whole of North Wales.

If only that were possible...

K. E. HEATON

CHAPTER 1

Saturday, 23rd, April 1955.

Chorley town center in the county of Lancashire U.K.

In an age when most individuals had never even heard the term supermarket, many of John Bingham's older, regular customers would call at his butchers shop every two or three days to purchase their meat. They expected and subsequently received the big mans personal attention and he in turn could count on their loyalty to come back week after week. With only a handful of people having ownership of a refrigerator, it was a lot safer to buy their beef, lamb and in particular pig products on a regular basis to avoid the obvious dangers of food poisoning. They'd store it in the pantry below stairs in the coolest part of the house, but when summer arrived and daily temperatures increased, the local piggy's would get a temporary stay of execution with customers reluctant to buy it if there wasn't an R in the month.

And for anyone who'd ever been to the high street butcher before, there was always the wonderful expectation of a second even more memorable visit. It was a combination of factors that brought people back time and time again, but the moment they stepped over the threshold and shuffled their feet through several inches of fresh sawdust. The slaughterer would enrich their experience with a display of knife craft only possible by a true artisan. And although most humans are predominately visual foragers the odor of raw meat was also a temptation that a lot of John Bingham's customers found very hard to resist. Especially now after fourteen years of food rationing, and despite the fact the country was on its knees, if you could find the money, you could have what you wanted.

The man himself would be standing behind the counter with his bloodstained blue and white striped apron. A thick leather belt hung loosely around his middle weighted down on one flank by a scabbard of carefully selected blades and the unmistakable tools of the abattoir.

And inevitably huge sides of beef would be hanging down on either side of the man from a giant rail suspended close to the ceiling. So whilst numerous younger rather slimmer members of staff would scurry around behind him in a vane attempt to curry favor with the boss. It was business as usual, and the only difference on this particular day was the presence a young lad called Robert Rudd out shopping with his mother who experienced for the very first time such extravagant scenes of creative butchery that he was completely captivated by everything he could see. And hardly any wonder as the butcher's skills were on display in full view of the customers proving yet again how proficient Bingham had become. Often he'd remind people "I've spent the best part of my life behind the knife." Bingham would declare. Although unsurprisingly a few of the punters, and not always as one might expect the little old ladies with their thick stockings and matching grey hair were chilled by the visions of his work. It wasn't everyone's understanding of a great day out and despite their willingness to devour his carefully prepared products many were not too enthusiastic about witnessing the butcher's masterly incisions. Young master Rudd however with his black curly hair and face full of freckles was not one of those. Unashamedly the boy found great satisfaction as he watched the big man split the dead animal in half longitudinally before removing the prime cuts from the carcass and then subsequently proceeding to bone and trim his handiwork with all the skills and dexterity at his disposal. In recent months Jack Rudd had taken nine year old Robert to see Victor Mature in "Demetrius and the Gladiators" at the Odeon cinema, and from what the boy could remember, Bingham's work reminded him of a scene from the movie. He longed to be able to use a knife in the same skillful way and have his own entourage to impress, and he wanted to be just like the butcher with his large muscular forearms that were not dissimilar to Popeye's, and his powerful stature. He remembered his first school-visit to the public swimming baths the previous week. How ashamed he'd been of his own nakedness and angry at being forced to reveal his thin scrawny arms in front of his classmates. And therefore it didn't take much imagination to realize how big and strong he actually could be…if only he were the butcher's boy.

"What's it going to be Missus?" Said the butcher confidently. "If its Sunday roast you're after?"

"No…no thank you." Robert's mum was quick to answer. "I'll have half a pound of shin beef please, if you don't mind?"

"Okay ma'am." Said the big man. "And is there anything else?"

"No that's alright thank you." She insisted. "But if you've got a bone for the dog please?"

"Yes of course missus." The butcher answered. "That's just a shilling then."

"Thank you." Said Missus Rudd as she paid the man. "Good day."

"Are we getting a dog mum…are we…when?" Robert asked eagerly as his mum shoved him out of the shop, back on to the street.

The butcher smiled.

"That's the last time. The very last time." Missus Rudd insisted.

"What?" Robert protested. "I don't understand mum, what have I done?"

"You." She said angrily. "I think you do it on purpose."

"I don't know what you mean?" Robert complained. "Honest!"

Missus Rudd grabbed the boy by his arm rather roughly and dragged him off along High Street towards the church. They climbed the hill rather quickly and immediately they'd got themselves around the back of Saint Mary's they slumped down on to a bench near to the remembrance garden.

"You don't get it, do you son?" Kathy Rudd insisted. "Me and your dad, we've tried really hard to make ends meet, do you understand?"

"Yeah I know." Said Robert sheepishly. "I'm sorry mum."

"Its not your fault, its not. I know that." She stressed. "But it doesn't help, does it? When you embarrass me like that?"

"It won't happen again mum." Robert threw his arms around her waist. "I promise."

Kathy was a small somewhat plain unremarkable woman but make no mistake having lived through years of hardship and typical of most young women in post war Britain she was very proud. She had short mousy brown hair and no distinguishing features, just another Northern lass who never complained and kept her opinions to herself. Not unattractive by any means but this was a time of austerity and there was little enough money to go around on day-to-day necessities without wasting it on such trivial things as make up. And as most married women in particular were bereft of any sort of beauty products to enhance their features, Kathy wasn't alone. She was trim, slightly undernourished but nevertheless remarkably healthy. Would seldom use any sort of public transport and subsequently walked everywhere she went. But despite even a brisk walk her pale complexion, although not clinically significant, would always make her appear slightly ill or tired. There may have been an explosion of bright bold lip color on the cinema screens from pouting movie stars like Grace

Kelly or Marilyn Monroe. But scarce evidence of that could be found on the streets of Chorley in 1955 and therefore apart from a handful of girls armed with a little rouge and black mascara most womenfolk including Robert's mum were desperate to improve their lot.

"I've got myself a job love." She announced suddenly. "It had to be done."

"Why?" Said Robert painfully.

"Because…" His Mum answered. "We need the money, it's as simple as that."

"Does Dad know?"

"Yeah he does." She acknowledged. "He's not happy about it, as you can well imagine. Reckons it'll make him a laughing stock with all his mates at work. You know what he's like, he wants a good little wife to stay at home and see to the house."

"So…what's going to happen then?" Asked Robert worriedly.

"How do you mean?"

"With me, and school?" Said Robert.

"Well…you're going to have to learn to be a bit more independent aren't you Robert?" She insisted. "And grow up!"

Robert thought long and hard, his mum had caught him by surprise. He didn't want her to go out to work, he was sure of that, but he did have friends whose mothers were already working and they seemed to survive okay.

"Where's the job?" Said Robert eventually. "Is it local?"

"Guess?" She insisted.

"I bet it's the laundry. Isn't it?" Robert smiled confidently. "That's where David Sumner's mum works.

"No it's not the laundry." She laughed. "But you are very close."

"Witter's carpets?" Robert shouted loudly. "Yeah. That'll be it."

"No. Wrong again." Kathy insisted. "I'll tell you…shall I? And put you out of your misery. It's the pie shop on Eaves Lane. I start on Monday!"

"The pie shop?" Shouted Robert excitedly. "That's brilliant mum."

"You reckon?" Kathy grinned.

"Definitely." Robert insisted. "And will they let you take all the pies home, that they haven't managed to sell?"

"I doubt it." Said Kathy. "You know what old Mister Burtons like, he probably hangs on to them for some strange reason. I can't imagine him giving anything away?"

"No you're right mum." Said Robert. "He even sells off all the old broken biscuits at three-pence a bag, so there's not much chance of a free pie…is there?"

"That's true." Kathy agreed. "But it does mean that we might manage a few days away at wakes weeks?"

"Really?" Said Robert excitedly. "Blackpool?"

"We'll see." Kathy smiled. "It all depends?"

"On what?" Robert demanded.

"On whether we can make the extra money stretch that far?"

"You will mum. Won't you?" Robert insisted. "I know you will."

"Don't build your hopes up." Said Kathy. "Nothings definite, not yet anyway, but listen, even if Blackpool doesn't happen. You'll get away for a few weeks. I promise."

"How come?" Said Robert cautiously.

"Well. After wakes week's, everything gets back to normal. Doesn't it?" Kathy smiled. "The schools are still closed for another four weeks, and I'll be back at work. Someone's got to look after you."

"Go on. Tell me?" Robert frowned. "Who have you got to come and stay with us?"

"No one Robert." Said Kathy seriously. "We've booked you a train ticket to North Wales. You're going to spend the rest of the summer at Grandpa Gerald's. You'll love it there!"

Jack Rudd worked as a maintenance electrician at the Royal Ordnance Factory at Euxton, only a few miles from Chorley town center. He was on regular monthly shift work, usually two weeks of mornings followed by a week of afternoons and then subsequently a week of nights. He expected and was offered his two weeks annual leave during wakes weeks when every industrial North West town would close down completely and anyone who could afford it, would head for the coast. Originally a religious celebration or feast that developed in to a secular holiday during the industrial revolution and by the nineteen fifties was still going strong. In Scotland the equivalent period was called the Trades Fortnight" when for two weeks every summer the tradesmen would take their holidays. But it was a perfect time for all the factory owners to get their house in order and see to all the overdue maintenance jobs that couldn't be done when machines were running flat out during the rest of the year. And for that very reason, Jack's employers had also offered him an incentive to work through wakes weeks, surrender his summer entitlement and double his pay for two weeks.

So. If he was ever going to save up enough money to put down as a deposit on a new property and get him and his young family out of the council house, now was the time.

Therefore as the last two weeks of July began and seemingly everyone else apart from the Rudd's had packed their bags ready for the seaside, Robert was at home in the garden. He wanted a game of soccer and normally played in goal, but with no one to play with, he kicked his football against the back wall of the washhouse in such a reckless manner, it was inevitable when one of the windows came crashing in.

"You stupid boy." Kathy screamed at the top of her voice. "How many times have I told you?" She added. "Just wait until your father gets in."

CHAPTER 2

So as expected Robert did get a lecture when Jack came in from work but it was mainly for Kathy's benefit, to appease her and reinforce what she'd already said to the boy. Jack Rudd had broken a few windows of his own over the years and not always by accident, and because he'd denied his son the chance of getting away to Blackpool if only for a few days, Jack preferred to go easy on the lad. What he and Kathy had decided to do made good financial sense and hopefully if they secured a foot on the property ladder, it was a small price to pay. But nevertheless immediately he saw the other kids in the street chasing about excitedly, the boys with their recent short back and sides and the girls in their new summer clothes, Jack felt terribly guilty.

Kathy had every intention of taking Robert away for the odd day trip to Southport or maybe even Scarborough if either Tom Jackson or Cliff Owens coaches were not fully booked, but it wasn't the same as actually going on holiday. On most day trips to the seaside, the coach drivers would set off from Chorley Flat Iron Market about nine, arrive at their destination about lunch time and arrange to pick up all the punters again about six o' clock. So when all the real holidaymakers were heading back to their boarding houses and hotels for evening meal, the day-trippers were already homeward bound. And even though the nineteen fifties coaches were a darned sight more reliable than the opened top char-a-banc's from the early part of the twentieth century, they were still incredibly uncomfortable, vehicle suspension was not particularly sophisticated and the motorway network was nonexistent.

For those wishing to sunbathe on the many different beaches around the British Isles however the July weather did not disappoint, and so for Robert and his mum it was somewhat galling that as most of their neighbors joined the mass exodus to the coast, the temperatures rocketed.

And because it didn't rain on St Swithun's day, as far as most Lancastrians believed it wouldn't rain again for at least forty days.

A difficult time for young Robert when all he wanted was a white-knuckle ride on Blackpool Pleasure Beach, an opportunity to build sandcastles and a leisurely trot along the beach on one of Blackpool's famous donkeys.

Unfortunately though, at least for this particular year…it was not to be.

When Kathy checked availability with the coach operators the only trips they could book was one to Skipton in North Yorkshire and on another day Bowness-on-Windermere in the Lake District.

Both of them would be an escape and new adventure but it wasn't what the boy wanted.

The day trip to Yorkshire was the first excursion that mother and son would embark upon and when they arrived in Skipton the market was in full swing and located at the very heart of town. Each of the traders erected their own stalls above cobbled areas on either side of the High Street and very quickly crammed them full of goods. It was a complete contradiction to what was on offer during the war years and full of summer delicacies. Huge boxes of strawberries and raspberries were in abundance but then again so were bananas, an exotic treat that no one had seen in the nineteen forties and according to some, a fruit that many of the younger children had to be taught how to eat. And unsurprisingly with British defense spending still around nine per cent of GDP there was also a plethora of ex-army uniforms on offer and all the paraphernalia associated with anything remotely military.

As for the toy stalls they were also well stocked with a huge choice of footballs, hula-hoops and skipping ropes plus the countries current favorite…namely Play-Dough modeling clay.

Most of the items were of no interest to Robert. He already owned a football seemingly to everyone's disappointment and as far as he was concerned playing with hula-hoops was for girls. There was however one item that the boy found irresistible and that was a decent five-blade penknife with a wooden handle.

Kathy had said to him as they clambered off the coach that if he saw something that wasn't too expensive, she would consider treating him. It was either that or an hour's cruise in a narrow boat along the Leeds Liverpool Canal and if that didn't appeal to him, she'd promised to buy tickets for the castle.

Robert had no intention of climbing aboard one of those dirty, smelly little boats at the canal basin, but did have an inclination to visit the old castle. He was well aware that money was tight and realized that if he asked for the knife, that it would only cause trouble and so in the blink of an eye, he picked up two of the knives and held them both in one hand. Robert turned his hand over ensuring that one of the items remained firmly in his palm, the other he allowed to slip between his fingers as if he was still examining the piece. And then very deliberately he positioned that particular knife back on to the stallholder's counter, the other penknife still within his grasp as he placed both hands back into his pockets. The market trader and Robert's mum were both completely oblivious to what the boy had done. The whole maneuver had taken but a few seconds yet the way in which the boy had executed the theft was so precise and simple, one might think that he'd done that sort of thing before.

It was hot so they dawdled across town in the direction of the castle, sat down on an old wooden bench at the side of Holy Trinity Church and tucked in to their salmon paste sandwiches.

"Some people." Said Kathy suddenly. "They get all the sunshine…have you noticed?"

"I don't understand mum?" Robert answered. "Who do you mean, like the cowboys in the wild west?"

"No. Doesn't matter where you live." Kathy insisted. "And I'm not talking about the weather."

Robert looked confused.

They waltz through life, a lot of them." She added. "They've not a care in the world, while most of us end up living in the shadows. Its not right son is it?"

"No it's not mum." Robert agreed. "But you know what? We've all got sunshine today, even the poor people."

Robert's mum laughed…it was strange really because at the same time he could have sworn she had tears in her eyes.

"So listen." She insisted suddenly. "As you grow up Robert, you need to be strong. Make sure you get what you want, and don't let anyone push you into the shadows…ever…do you hear?"

"Yeah. I hear you mum." Said the boy.

"Good…" She growled. "And don't let me down.

"I won't mum…" Robert assured her. "…I promise."

From the minute he stepped through the castle gatehouse, Robert was captivated. Built in 1090 by a Norman Baron named Robert de Romille, Skipton castle was one of the most complete fully roofed medieval castles in England. The building had survived for almost a millennium, had endured a turbulent history and despite having been besieged for three long years during the English Civil War was still in amazing condition. Within the outer curtain wall were other enclosed areas and subsidiary buildings including the ruins of a twelfth century chapel, and in the very center a tudor courtyard.

Robert was able to run around at will and explore every nook and cranny. The boy like his mother had big ambitions and imagined himself as a great king in complete control of everyone and everything that he could see. From the top of the watchtower to the very depths of the dungeon, if only for a short period of time…he Robert Rudd was the new owner and undisputed ruler of this particular fortress. And as far as little Robert was concerned, buoyed up by Kathy's earlier comments and with a shiny new knife in his pocket…he was in charge.

He promised himself that one day, when he was older somehow he'd make damned sure that he owned a place just like this with all its history, its splendor and magnificence. Okay he might have been born to a poor family in a deprived part of the country but one day…yes…one day everyone would have to sit up and take notice.

Later on however as they exited the castle a big chubby girl with long blonde hair and ruddy red cheeks bumped into Robert and all but knocked him off his feet. Compared to all her friends she was a huge kid, very intimidating and just like Medusa with a nest of venomous snakes protruding from her head, the fat girl had what appeared to be living braided pigtails that whirled around her as she moved. She never said sorry but she did laugh and then immediately set off again to join her mates.

"You're an idiot." Robert shouted after her and then whispered under his breath "Fatso."

"Get lost brat." She answered angrily. "Or I'll come back and punch you."

"You'll do no such thing." Kathy intervened. "Now go on…clear off." She insisted as she watched the girl waddle off towards her friends.

"Don't worry son." Kathy whispered confidently. "She's not worth bothering with, just forget all about it. It never happened."

"I will mum." Said Robert. "But I promise you this, if I ever do see her again, I'll have her thrown into the dungeons."

They both laughed.

Two days later and the intrepid pair of mother and son were off again, heading North in search of yet another adventure. In the Lake District there'd be no opportunity to visit medieval castles, but there was every chance of a proper boat trip on England's largest natural lake. When they'd visited Skipton in North Yorkshire, Robert had no inclination to climb aboard one of the narrow boats for a cruise along the Leeds Liverpool Canal, but when he saw the elegant steamers waiting at the slipway at Bowness-on-Windermere, suddenly he had an urge to take to the water.

Likely as not, it was the sleek white lines of the old coal fired steam yacht that grabbed the young lad's attention as they rushed towards the pier.

The "Swift" had been in service on Lake Windermere for over fifty years, ferrying passengers back and forth along England's most famous stretch of water. Costing £9,500 in 1900 she'd been expensive, but in the long-term a great investment. At a push she could still achieve a top speed of fifteen knots and often at the height of a summer season, with as many as 781 passengers on board, the old boat was indispensible. She had many distinctive features but none as prominent as the huge smokestack located mid-ship, and was easily recognizable from the other vessels that crisscrossed the lake with heartwarming regularity.

As Robert charged up the gangway in an effort to grab the best possible seats on top, Kathy handed over her well-earned pennies securing two return tickets to the Waterhead pier at Ambleside. And once aboard, the boy proceeded to throw him-self full length across the wooden slats of a steamer bench that doubled up as a storage compartment for one of the life rafts. It was a close call, only a few seconds later and a pair of rough looking scallywags from Liverpool would have claimed it for themselves, but before they had chance to complain, Robert's mum sat herself down alongside him.

"Well done love." She smiled. "Wow look at those flags."

It was quite gusty and as Robert turned his back on the would-be interlopers he looked up at the bunting that stretched from bow to stern, and watched it fluttering and dancing in the breeze. Each of the red, white and blue swallowtails was flapping around independently in no particular sequence as a light wind blew shoreward from the center of the lake.

"He's just a woolly back." Said the biggest kid. "He's a divvy."

Robert turned about to face the lads, but as he did so, they ran off towards the rear of the boat.

Kathy grabbed him immediately sensing that her boy was about to charge after them, but she needn't have worried, he'd got the best seat in the house, and that was all that mattered.

"What did he call me?" Robert looked puzzled.

"A woolly back." Kathy laughed. "Trust me, its not worth getting upset about."

"Why? What does it mean?" The boy asked.

"Its just an expression." She reassured him. "Its their description for anyone that doesn't come from Liverpool. Okay?"

"If you say so." Robert sighed. "But I'd still like to know what it means?"

"Its slang." Said Kathy. "It comes from the docklands in Liverpool. It's a word, that's all. It describes someone from out of town who comes in and gets a job unloading the ships."

"Really?" Said Robert sounding even more inquisitive. "But why am I a woolly back?"

"Because you've taken one of their jobs and they've seen you carrying bales of wool on your back and now your clothes are full of wool. Its as simple as that." She insisted.

Robert frowned.

"Oh I get it." He announced suddenly. "I grabbed the seat before they did, didn't I? And they were mad weren't they? And that's why they called me a woolly back. That's right isn't it mum?"

"Yeah that's right love." Kathy agreed. "So why don't we forget it now son. Shall we? And lets enjoy the sail."

There was a long pause in conversation as one of the deckhands lifted up the gangway and prepared to cast off. The hawsers were untied and gradually everyone on board became aware of the steady chugging sound from the old steam engine. The boat began to rock gently from side to side and all eyes watched excitedly as the old yacht slipped away ever so carefully from the side of the pier.

"Mum?" Asked Robert curiously.

"Yes son?" Said Kathy.

"What's a divvy?"

CHAPTER 3

It's a challenge for anyone who sails Lake Windermere for the very first time, to be unimpressed by the spectacular mountains, secluded bays and numerous wooded islands along the way.

And exactly as Kathy had predicted, her own handsome little boy with his black curly hair, long skinny arms and face full of freckles, was no exception.

Now in open water they'd left a myriad of other much smaller vessels behind them, a flotilla of tiny craft that bobbed about in the shallows close to the shore. Would-be mariners and inexperienced landlubber's who didn't care or dare to venture too far out into the middle of the lake. A few of them, mainly rowing boats, had tried to keep up with the "Swift" as she increased her speed and headed North, but inevitably had floundered in the old girl's wake.

And as the yacht picked up speed and made its way to the center of the lake, Robert hung over the grab rail at the edge of the deck. He watched the bow as it cut through the water with such precision, and it reminded him of John Bingham's cleaver as it sliced through a huge side of beef. The strength of the wind however was much stronger away from the shoreline and decidedly chilly and it was then that Kathy put her arm around the child to protect him from the elements. The seagulls continued to circle overhead and squawked frantically, determined to chase every morsel of food that any of the passengers might toss in their direction, as if their very lives depended on it.

Robert snuggled up to his mum as closely as he possibly could. It was necessary, but still, he couldn't ever remember wanting to be hugged as badly as he did at that moment.

Up until then, he'd never realized how much he needed her and the extent to which he sought her approval, but all of a sudden, it was obvious.

Almost twelve miles in length and a mile at its widest, Windermere is a ribbon lake that lies in a steep-sided pre-glacial river valley. It's the longest lake in England and at certain locations over two hundred feet deep. At least that's what it said on the back of Kathy's ticket, but as far as she and Robert was concerned, all that really mattered was the beauty of the place and how her relationship with Robert would be shaped by the day's events and their overwhelming desire to spend it together.

As the wind picked up and temperatures fell, more of the passengers made their way inside in search of warmth. It left only the diehards on top and consequently apart from a few small groups of people huddled together, the top deck was virtually deserted. Kathy and Robert decided to stay put and likewise an elderly gentleman with his lady companion decided to do the same. The old couple appeared very much at home in these surroundings, and despite it being summer they'd dressed like the weather might change at any minute.

The old chap looked very distinguished in his tweed jacket, burgundy coloured waistcoat and baggy corduroy trousers. He had a pair of large silvery whiskers that extended down the sides of his face, very neat and very defined.

And not to be outdone, his partner was also very well heeled. She too had a tweed jacket with black velvet collar, a knee-length navy skirt and a pair of long black leather boots with a fancy buckle. And to take her outfit up a notch she wore a kingfisher blue silk scarf around her neck and a black brushed-wool hat with feather trim.

So unless Kathy was mistaken, these were country folk of some social standing, who very likely owned and lived in a large rural property somewhere in the Lakes.

It was however complete conjecture on Kathy's part, and just a game that she would often play in situations like these, in order to pass the time. Meanwhile completely unaware of his mother's hypothesis and still sheltering from the cold like a baby chick, Robert peered out from under Kathy's gabardine and as he looked up, the old man caught his eye. The chap seemed quite pleased that he'd got the boy's attention and as far as Robert could tell there was a definite hint of mischief in his smile.

The boy returned the gesture with a big broad grin undeniably fascinated with his new admirer. It was the whiskers that did it, that and the old guy's impish, irresistible gaze.

"Don't stare Robert." Kathy whispered softly. "Its not nice."

"I'm not mum." Robert pleaded. "Honest."

"He's fine." The old man insisted. "He's a good looking boy."

"Thank you." Kathy smiled. "He's a bit cold. I'm trying to get him warm."

"I understand." The man nodded. "It can get a bit chilly up here."

"Why, have you done this sail before?" Kathy asked. "…On Lake Windermere?"

"Every week." He grinned. "For the past forty years, give or take."

"Oh right." Kathy tried to sound surprised. "So… hardly unexpected then?"

"Its always cold out on the water." The old lady interjected in a somewhat haughty almost condescending manner. "Even in the summer, its never any different."

The comment might have brought closure to the conversation, had fate not played its part. But immediately she turned away and the yacht changed course to an Easterly direction. A sudden squall encircled the old boat. A plume of white spray swept over the bow, and a huge gust of wind howled eerily across the upper deck.

At this point everyone was startled, even the old woman. She reached out instinctively to try and catch the very expensive brushed-wool hat with feather trim as it prepared for lift-off, but the effort was all in vain. It took to the air in a mini whirlwind way beyond her reach and unless some kind of miracle might occur, it was destined to end up in the lake.

And that's where young Robert came to the rescue. All those misspent summer evenings on Harpers Lane Rec playing football instead of doing his homework. All that diving around in goal, all that effort, it was only right, that one day, it would all prove worthwhile.

In the blink of an eye he emerged from the cocoon that Kathy had provided and leapt skyward in pursuit of the hat. He almost grabbed it at the first opportunity but at the very moment his fingers were closing in, another draft of air ensnared it and hurled it forward towards the front of the vessel.

He chased it frantically conscious of the fact that if it left the outer edges of the boat and blew away over the water, the chance was she would never get it back. It hovered for a while at least ten feet above the boy then forged ahead yet again until at long last it reached the bow. But at the very last moment, when the object was destined to be swept away and impossible to retrieve, the wind dropped ever so slightly. And as the hat descended towards the lake, Robert reached out beyond the grab-rail and snatched it from what would have been certain ruin.

"Bravo." Shouted the old lady as she hauled herself up. "What a magnificent performance…" She added. "Well done boy!"

Robert strolled back towards her looking ever so confident with him self. He stopped a few paces short of reaching her and in recognition of the applause from all the remaining passengers he gave a bow.

"I think this might be yours missus?" He smiled.

"Marvelous." Said the old man. "Absolutely marvelous. What a great effort."

"Thank you Sir." Said Robert modestly. "I was lucky."

"No!" Said the man. "That wasn't luck. You're a very clever young man… do you know that?"

Robert grinned.

"What you did then." The old chap insisted. "Was very brave and very skillful. And apart from anything else you've saved me a fortune."

Robert looked puzzled.

"Oh yes." The man assured him. "You wouldn't believe how much that hat cost?"

The old lady made a gesture with her hand for Kathy to come closer, and when she did, the woman whispered very gently in her ear.

"Am I allowed to treat the boy?" She sighed.

"It really isn't necessary." Said Kathy. "He'd have done the same for anyone."

"I know. I'm sure he would." The lady agreed. "But still, I'd like to give him something?"

Kathy shrugged her shoulders.

"If you must." She smiled. "But honestly, you don't need to."

"Thank you." Said the woman as she leaned forward and grasped the boy's hand. "Please… take this son. You deserve it."

Robert turned to look at Kathy and at the same time unclenched his fist very, very slowly. His face said it all. He recognized what it was, but he'd never held a ten-shilling note before.

"No please." Kathy insisted. "That's too much. Seriously."

"Nonsense." Said the woman quite dismissively. "He's earned it, and now I've made my mind up, I can't take no for an answer."

"Thank you." Said Robert quite swiftly before his mum had chance to put in yet another objection. "Thank you very much."

"You're welcome." The lady insisted. "Now… come and sit yourself down alongside me. Let's get to know each other?"

It soon dawned on the intrepid day-trippers, that their new acquaintances were a lot more interesting than what they first thought. The name Pennington was nothing special in Chorley, but in the Lake District it carried a lot more prominence.

The old couple introduced themselves as Allen and Elizabeth, husband and wife for the past thirty years. Somehow he'd survived the Great War and at the ripe old age of thirty-nine had come back home and opened his own butcher's shop in Ambleside. They lived in the village of Grasmere, about four miles north of town, in a large detached cottage. A property they'd managed to secure in 1919, for the princely sum of three hundred and twenty five pounds.

"Is it a castle?" Asked Robert excitedly. "I love castles, and one day… I'm going to own one."

"Not exactly." The old man shook his head. "But if things had been a little different?"

How so?" The boy was curious.

"Life's not always fair son." Said Pennington sounding rather irritated. "Things have a way of going wrong. And some people don't always get what they're entitled to. Do you understand?"

"I do." Robert insisted. "Mum and I have had the same conversation. She said that some people get to live in the sunshine all the time and others have to live in the shadows."

Kathy smiled.

"She's right." The man acknowledged. "That's exactly how it is."

"Why?" Robert asked very politely. "Is your house always in the shadows?"

"The house is lovely. " Said the man dolefully. "In fact it's a very beautiful house and I'm very, very lucky… but?"

"But what?" The boy was captivated. He just couldn't help himself and was literally hanging on to the old man's every word.

"There is another property in the Lake District. Its about thirty miles away from here." The man explained. "Its what I call my ancestral home, somewhere that I like to visit now and again. Although every time I go there, I come away feeling even more despondent, even more depressed."

"Is it a castle?" Robert demanded to know. "Is it?"

"It is Robert." Said the man proudly. "Muncaster Castle! Do you know it?"

Robert had to admit that he'd never heard of it. But he did say that if it was anything like Skipton Castle, it must be very special.

"Its very old." Said Pennington. "Not quite as old as Skipton, as far as I can remember, but still, its steeped in history and a beautiful place to live."

"Was it yours?" The boy just had to ask.

"No unfortunately not." The old man had to admit. "But if I'd been around in 1917 when Baron Muncaster died, things might have been different."

"Were you related?" Kathy dared to ask.

"I was my dear." Pennington nodded. "And it's alright knowing something. But often... it's a devil trying to prove it."

"You had a claim?" Kathy urged him on. "On the estate?"

"Without question." He answered. "Although at the time, all I was really interested in, was trying to survive the carnage on the Western Front. And I have to admit the last thing on my mind was what might be happening back at home. It all seemed so far away, and by the time I got back, everything was done and dusted. That's just the way it is."

"You were robbed." Said Robert emphatically.

"Steady on son." Said Kathy. "Mister Pennington doesn't want to hear that."

"No. The boy's right." Said the old lady. "He was robbed. But there's nothing we can do about it."

As they neared the shore, the unique architectural style of Waterhead pier came into view, the wind subsided and for the first time in ages, the sun came shining through.

CHAPTER 4

Ambleside is almost a mile from the Waterhead pier and as visitors step off the boat, they have an option to jump on a local bus, hire a taxi or walk into town.

Kathy had decided on the latter, she and Robert would stretch their legs but more importantly it would save money.

The time had come to say goodbye to the old couple, but before she had chance to say anything, old Mister Pennington stepped closer.

"Have you made any plans for lunch?" He asked endearingly.

"No. Not really." Kathy was taken aback somewhat. "I normally bring sandwiches. But we've decided to have a change today and eat out."

"Excellent." The old man smiled. "Then you must come with us."

"No. I'm afraid not." Kathy hesitated. "We've only got a limited amount of time before heading back."

"And what time do you sail dear?" His wife asked very sweetly.

"At five." Said Kathy. "The coach leaves Bowness at seven o' clock."

"Well. It's up to you of course." Said Pennington. "But if you'll let me buy you some lunch at the Salutation Hotel in Ambleside, I'd be more than happy. It'll only take us half an hour or so, to get served, and then you'd still have the rest of the afternoon to yourselves. What do you think? Are you up for it?"

Kathy only had to look at Robert's face to know what he was thinking. He liked the old man and the thought of eating out at some big fancy hotel was an opportunity he didn't want to miss.

"That would be lovely." Kathy agreed. "That's very kind of you. Thank you so much."

"It's our pleasure." The old chap insisted. "Isn't that right Elizabeth?"

"Absolutely." Said his wife. "I couldn't agree more."

As they exited the pier and stepped away from the old wooden structure, there was still the issue of transport and how Mister Pennington intended for them all to get to the hotel. Kathy was quite prepared to walk into town as originally planned but doubted whether Missus Pennington was able to hike that far. The old lady was rather tiny and a little unsteady on her feet, but in the end it didn't matter. The old butcher had a plan.

To the right of the jetty was an open-top horse drawn carriage waiting patiently in the midday sun. An elegant Victorian landau with enough seating for four passengers, a separate raised bench-seat for the driver, and two frisky black stallions harnessed up front.

"Okay. That's the answer." The old man smiled. "Come on Robert. Climb up. Show us how it's done."

The boy didn't need telling twice that's for sure, and a few minutes later they were all onboard and heading into town. And as they left the pier behind them, they passed many of their fellow passengers walking briskly in the same direction. There were lots of familiar faces on the busy pavement, but two in particular stood out from the crowd. A couple of young scallywags from Liverpool that didn't look too happy when they saw young Robert racing by in a beautiful horse drawn carriage, like one of the cowboys in the wild west. No doubt wondering why some people have to live in the shadows whilst others seemed to have all the luck.

And the Salutation Hotel was yet another example of how the other half lived, a lovely provincial hotel that occupied an elevated location in the center of town, and the likes of which, young Robert had never seen. The establishment had remained open to businessmen and travellers for almost three hundred years. It had a lintel over the door with a date of 1656, only six years after Ambleside was granted its market charter. Originally a farmhouse where the farmer's wife provided ale for thirsty visitors, and once in a while, a rough bed in the hayloft for any customers, who'd drank a few too many.

As the local market thrived selling mainly wool and cloth, Ambleside prospered, and consequently so did the "Salutation."

By 1955 the hotel was lavishly decorated and very tasteful.

And as old Mister Pennington led the way to his favorite corner of the restaurant, the others followed obediently in his footsteps. Robert stroked each antique chair very gently with his fingers as they ambled by, taking in as much of this new environment as he possibly could. The fragrance from the freshly cut flowers on each and every table and the soft almost whispered orchestral music in the background. The boy had never been in such opulent surroundings, but knew instinctively, it was where he belonged.

"So. What's it going to be young man?" Pennington grinned. "Take a look at the menu. You can have whatever you want."

"Please. Don't encourage him." Kathy insisted. "Its very expensive."

"Maybe so." Said the old chap. "But once in a while, we've got to push the boat out. It's a special occasion."

"It feels like someone's birthday." Said Robert thoughtfully.

"I couldn't agree more." Said Pennington. "That's exactly how I feel."

"Well. Its very good of you to treat us." Kathy smiled. "And we are very grateful."

"You needn't be." The old man stressed. "We're all friends here, and I can't think of anyone else I'd like to celebrate with."

Suddenly everyone looked rather puzzled, everyone apart from Pennington himself that is. Even his wife looked a little mystified.

"You got it in one Robert." He announced excitedly. " And I have to say, that was very astute of you. You are of course absolutely right. It is someone's birthday today… mine!"

For a few moments at least you could have heard a pin drop, that or anything else that dared to break the silence.

"Wow." Kathy gasped as she reached across the table to shake his hand. "That is a surprise. Congratulations."

"Thank you." Pennington smiled. "Yes. And it's a big one."

"A big one?" Robert asked as he followed his mum's example and grasped the man's hand. "How big?"

"Well. I can't deny it." The man was all smiles. "It doesn't get much bigger."

Once again, everyone waited eagerly for Pennington's reply.

"I was born in the year of our lord 1055." The old man suddenly declared. "I know. It's hard to believe isn't it? But there you go. That's what happens if you look after yourself."

The boy giggled.

"Just ignore him." His wife insisted. "My husband is just being silly. He was born in 1880 and yes it is his birthday, but despite what he might tell you Robert, he's only seventy five."

Kathy laughed nervously. "So. It is a big one!" She declared.

"Definitely." Said Pennington as he grabbed hold of a waiter by his coat tails quite unceremoniously. "We'll have some champagne please." He insisted. "And whatever my guests might like to order."

"Of course Sir." Said the young attendant. "I'll get straight onto it."

The Rudd's never ate out, and so, it came as a bit of shock when they started to read the hotel menu. The choice on offer was simply mind-blowing. Food rationing may have finished, but for most folks like Kathy and her boy, it would take a while before British culinary skills would improve. Up until then the meager choice of ingredients and flavorings had prevented even the best of cooks from creating cordon bleu dishes. The 1950's were the age of spam fritters, salmon paste sandwiches, tinned fruit and evaporated milk. And if you were lucky, fish on a Friday and ham salad on Sunday evening. The only possible way to add any real flavor to such bland cooking was with brown sauce or tomato ketchup.

In the end Kathy played it safe and ordered grilled sausages, grilled tomatoes and mashed potato. Missus Pennington had mulligatawny soup for starters followed by tinned salmon rissoles, creamed swede and once again a good helping of mash. Robert decided to be brave and took advice from the old man. He'd never tasted rabbit before, but when it arrived with a generous helping of braised onions and baked sliced potatoes, he tucked into it, as if he'd been eating it all his life. When it came to sweets however, the choice was a lot easier and unsurprisingly a unanimous decision was made, four very large portions of Jam Roly-Poly, each with a huge dollop of thick creamy custard. And, at the old mans insistence, a huge pot of breakfast tea to follow with a wonderful assortment of after dinner mints and chocolates.

For a young boy like Robert who despite his tender age, already recognized the huge differences between the haves and have not's, this was a day he would never forget. A day that he hoped would never end, and a day that he suspected would never have occurred, had someone not planned for it to happen.

Kathy assumed that as soon as the old man had settled the bill, that he and his good lady would want to head off home, but the truth was, they were enjoying themselves too much, and in no rush to go anywhere. And Robert was obviously intrigued by the man, fascinated by his storytelling and amused at the old chap's descriptions of every day events. The boy had always been a good listener, regardless of who might be telling a tale, but he'd never heard anyone quite like Pennington.

"I'll tell you what." Said the old man as they stepped outside and into the sunshine. "I fancy a stroll, anybody want to join me?"

"Why? What have you got in mind?" Elizabeth Pennington was well aware of her husband's foolhardy ideas. She wasn't getting any younger, and after a wonderful lunch, had no inclination to walk anywhere.

"Its obvious." Insisted the old chap. "Our route is clearly marked and it's right in front of our noses.

Everyone twirled around instinctively looking for some kind of clue, but not for long, and very quickly, all eyes turned back to the man with the whiskers.

"Stock Ghyll Force!" Pennington announced suddenly. "There's a path behind the Salutation Hotel. It'll take us ten minutes that's all. There's a huge waterfall Robert, you'll love it."

The smile on Robert's face was almost as remarkable as the huge frown on Missus Pennington's. And in fact, it wasn't a frown at all, more of a scowl. Not that her husband was paying much attention to her. He was too busy grinning at the boy.

"Allen." The old lady growled. "Is that really such a good idea?"

"I don't see why not?" He answered confidently. "The weathers good. And I'm sure this young man would enjoy it. But… only if Kathy agrees?"

"Yes." Said Kathy acceptingly. "If Robert would like to go with you, then I have no objections. Although I must be honest, and speaking only for myself of course, I think I'd prefer to stay here in town and take a look around."

"Now. That is a good idea." Missus Pennington smiled. "Let's do a bit of shopping you and I, and leave the menfolk to do whatever they want."

"Thanks mum." Robert screamed as he threw his arms around her. "I'll be good."

"You better." She insisted. "Okay. Be off with you. I'll see you later."

Stock Ghyll Force was a short walk from the center of Ambleside, an amazing series of waterfalls that tumble down the hillside and into town. A tributary of the River Rothay where once there were a dozen watermills, producing all kinds of things such as paper, bobbins, fabrics and predictably a huge amount of corn for the locals. And after all, this was arguably England's wettest place and notorious for its heavy rainfall, but not on this particular day. When Robert and Mister Pennington trekked up the mountain, the conditions were perfect, the path was unusually quiet and the views were spectacular.

CHAPTER 5

"Tell me this Robert." Said the old man curiously as he took a breather. "Do you believe in fate?"

"I'm not sure." Said Robert thoughtfully. "Should I?"

"Well. It all depends." Pennington pondered for a while. "Some things seem to happen just by chance. Have you ever noticed?"

"Yeah. I guess so." Said the boy. "Like today. When me and mum met you and Missus Pennington?"

"Yes." Pennington agreed. "That's a good example. So tell me this Robert. Was that fate or was it destiny?"

"I don't know." Said the boy. "What's the difference?"

"Its quite easy really." The old man insisted. "Fate is usually associated with a negative outcome. Whereas... destiny is often linked to something positive."

"The answers simple then." Robert smiled. "Meeting you and Missus Pennington. It was destiny."

The old chap put his arms around the boy and hugged him.

"I'm glad you think so Robert." He laughed. "And never forget… if you're not happy. Then all you have to do is change your destiny. So… come on, let's get ourselves up this mountain before the weather changes.

They made their way up the Ghyll and stopped frequently, and once at the top, slumped down on the grass for a long earned rest. No one spoke for a while. It took Pennington a while to start breathing normally again and the boy, although not particularly puffed, was happy just to lie back and enjoy the view.

"Robert..." Said the old man solemnly. "I have to tell you something. And I'm under no illusions. What I'm about to tell you will be very hard to understand and even harder to believe. But… to put it simply, our meeting today did not happen by chance. I orchestrated it, I planned the whole thing."

Robert raised his head then propped himself up on his elbows. He didn't say anything at first and for a while the old man wondered if the boy had even heard what he'd said. But then eventually, Robert pulled himself up even further and began to speak.

"Alright." He groaned looking more than a little confused. "So. Let's say I believe you. Why would you do that? You don't even know us?"

"But I do." Pennington insisted. "Master Robert Rudd… I know all about you!"

"Prove it then." Said Robert frustratingly.

"I don't know where to start." Said the old chap. "There's not enough time. But I'll tell you as much as I can, and after that, your dad will have to fill in all the details."

"My dad? What's my dad got to do with all this?" The boy was getting angry. "You don't even know him?"

"Who… Jack?" Insisted Pennington. "Trust me lad, I know Jack Rudd. I know everything. Where he lives. What he does for a job. And more importantly, where he came from. And I don't want to frighten you. I want you to trust me. But the big question is? What will you do with all this information? In the next few days, you're going to have to make some very important decisions. Are you up it? Only time will tell?"

"I'm not scared of anything or anybody." Said Robert defiantly. "So go ahead and tell me."

The old man sighed loudly.

"Okay. Here we go." He gasped. "If I can convince you that what I'm saying is true, then its up to you, to do the same for me, when next we meet. Do you understand?"

"No. Not really." Said the boy.

"I was born in the year 1055 in Calvados, Normandy, France." Pennington began. "Just like I said back at the hotel.

Missus Pennington thinks I'm very eccentric. And the thing is, I have tried to tell her the truth many times over the years, but unfortunately she choses not to listen. I don't criticize her for that however. She's a good woman.

But you Robert, you have a right to know the truth. Whether you accept my explanations of course are a different matter.

My original name is Robert of Rhuddlan. I was a Norman adventurer. Lord of North East Wales and for a period of time Lord of all North Wales. I was killed at Rhuddlan Castle in the county of Flint in the year 1093, during yet another one of those bloody Welsh uprisings. And apparently I had my head chopped off, according to the history books that is. But if there's one thing I've learned over the years, is that history is always written by the victor, regardless of the truth.

"But your name is Allen Pennington?" The boy persisted. "It doesn't make sense?"

"No. I know." The old man agreed. "And here comes the bit that Missus Pennington can never comprehend. Are you ready for this?"

Robert nodded.

"After the skirmish at Rhuddlan. I escaped and made my way back by boat to another of my castles on the Isle of Anglesey. Have you heard of Aberlleiniog?"

"No." Said the boy.

"Well." Said Pennington. "The old place looks a lot different now, but in those days, the sea came right in land and at high tide, the waves would crash against the castle walls. And at the base of the castle, exposed only at low water, was the strangest of voids. A deep crack in the Earths surface, at one moment it would be there, and the next, impossible to find. And I knew that despite certain people having entered this place before, but never seen again. With a hundred Welsh warriors closing in, and only a handful of men to defend the castle. I decided my own destiny, and I entered the cave. The incoming tide erased my footprints immediately and I wandered aimlessly into the abyss."

"That still doesn't explain things." Robert insisted. "So where did it take you?"

"I had heard a story, passed down by the old Welsh druids, that there was certain places where you could disappear and then reappear some time later in the future. I never believed such tales. I just assumed that it was some sort of fissure between the rocks, and all I had to do was to climb upwards away from the seawater, and that eventually I'd find my way out. At least that's what I thought." The old man sighed. "Then every so often, I'd see a flash of light up ahead and I rushed forward thinking that was the way out. But every time I got close, the light would dwindle and recede further into the hillside. And then suddenly it split into three. I didn't know what to do. So I made my choice. I dived forward straight ahead and before I knew it, I was out in the open. Only I wasn't at Aberlleiniog castle any more, I was up to my neck in mud. And I wasn't the only one.

I could hear others calling out for help, but no one came. I wasn't injured but I was well and truly stuck, and only for the corpse underneath me, I'd have disappeared into the ground yet again, and never re-emerged. Eventually under the protection of darkness, somehow, I crawled out and climbed onto a wooden duckboard, leaving every fragment of eleventh century clothing behind me. And almost immediately, I stumbled over a man's body, a soldier that had just been killed, fighting with the second battalion of the Border Regiment. It was April 1917 and I'd turned up at the battle of Arras close to Vimy Ridge. I undressed the man, put on his uniform, rolled him over into the mud and watched carefully as he disappeared slowly into the bog. And then all I had to do was crawl away towards the British lines. So Robert… can you guess the soldier's name?"

"Allen Pennington?" Robert whispered.

"Exactly." Said the old man. "And that's who I became."

"And no one questioned you?" Asked Robert suspiciously.

"No. No one." Pennington insisted. "I came back to Britain at the end of the war and headed for the Lake District. I had some evidence that Muncaster castle might be mine, a few letters from the old Baron and his wife, but not enough to risk putting my new identity on the line. I could never have proved it in court. The man had no brothers, sisters or parents. It was like he'd never existed. And so… I decided to leave it. I met Elizabeth, settled down in Grasmere, opened up the butcher's shop and the rest is history."

"And where does my dad come into all this?" Robert growled. "I still don't understand?"

"So…" Pennington sighed. "Only a year after I disappeared from under their very noses, the Welsh were still searching. Not only for me, but anyone connected with me, and in particular my offspring, most of who were still in the vicinity of Aberlleiniog. No one was safe, especially my youngest child. His name was John and in 1094 was two years old. If the rebels had found him, they would have killed him and therefore my eldest brother Gerald made a very brave decision, that he would try and find the same portal that I had used to escape a year earlier. He scoured the area and searched every day at low tide until eventually one particular day he found the opening. Immediately he grabbed the child and made his escape. Unlike me however, he did emerge from the cave close to Aberlleiniog in the year 1918.

And after concerns that some of the rebels might follow him, he moved to England and set up home in Lancashire in a busy industrial North West town. He registered the child as his own and gave him the name Jack. Jack Rudd."

"That sort of makes sense." Said Robert carefully. "And my granddad's name is Gerald. But…?"

"But what?" Asked the old man.

"Well." Said Robert. "If Jack is your son, and not Gerald's…?"

"Yes." The old man smiled.

"Then. You're my granddad aren't you?" Robert whispered.

"I am Robert." Said Pennington. "And I'm very proud of you."

"That." Said Robert. "Its the most ridiculous story I've ever heard."

"Perhaps." Said the old man. "But its true… every single word."

"So." Robert asked. "Why have you never been to see us? I'm nine years old and suddenly I've got a new Granddad? Why?"

"It was too complicated." Pennington insisted. "And apart from that, your Mum knows knowing about it. She's oblivious to any of this and in line with your Dad's wishes, she mustn't find out."

"Unless I tell her." Said the boy defiantly. "She's a right to know."

"Maybe she has." Said the old man. "Will she believe you?"

"I don't know." Robert whispered. "What harm could it do?"

"Well." Pennington insisted. "There may come a time when we have to tell her. But for the moment, your Dad thinks that would be very unwise."

"Why?" Robert shouted. "I still don't understand?"

"Because." The old man smiled. "There's a little job that we want you to do Robert…and if successful, will improve your life immediately, and for years to come. You'll get back what's rightfully yours. But like everything we do, it's not without risk. And the last thing we want is for you to have any additional pressures and for Kathy to prevent you from doing what's right."

"Is it very dangerous?" Asked the boy sharply.

"It depends." Said Pennington. "But put it this way. If your Dad and I didn't think that you were capable, we would never ask. And since we've met and I know now what sort of boy you are, I've every confidence. Jack told me you were fit and strong, and he was right."

"What do you want me to do? Tell me?" The boy insisted immediately.

"When you get home." Said the old chap. "Jack will tell you everything you need to know. It's all organized. And as you're probably aware, your train tickets to North Wales are already booked. Gerald will meet you as planned and yes he does know that we are having this conversation. In future he would prefer it if you addressed him as uncle, but whilst at home with your Mum and Dad, its better if you still refer to him as Granddad. Do you understand?"

"Yes… I understand." Said Robert loudly with more than a hint of mutiny in his voice. "Although I don't see how my new Uncle Gerald can help me. He's miserable. He's not very fit and he can't walk anywhere without a stick."

"I'll ignore you ever said that." Pennington growled. "Gerald could be the difference between success and failure. He's a very capable man despite his age, and without him, you can't do anything. And if there's one person you'll have to depend on. It's Gerald… he's the gatekeeper."

CHAPTER 6

As they made their way back down the Ghyll, their conversation was at an end. The boy was deep in thought and any euphoria he may have felt since meeting Pennington and his wife, had now been dashed. What the old chap had told him was the most implausible, absurd story that he'd ever heard. He was annoyed at Pennington and the way he'd spoken, and the fact that he knew all about him, and his family. He couldn't wait to get back on the boat and tell Kathy what had happened. But suddenly, as they reached the rear of the hotel, the old man stepped in front of the boy and stopped him, dead in his tracks.

"Take a deep breath son." Said Pennington. "You need to think this through."

"Oh yeah…. really?" Robert answered angrily. "Why's that then?"

"Well. If you don't." The old man insisted. "You… and Kathy and Jack, you're going to struggle, for the rest of your lives. You'll never have more than two halfpennies to rub together. Trust me."

"That's not true." Said Robert defiantly. "My mum's got a job now and we're going to buy a house… so there."

"I know. Jack told me." Said Pennington. "He's going to get a mortgage and borrow loads of money. I understand that. He wants to improve things for you and your mum. Why wouldn't he?"

"So. What's wrong with that?" Robert gasped.

"Nothing." Said the old guy. "Jack's a good man. But by the time he's finished paying all the money back. He'll be shattered and too old to enjoy it. It's not the answer. There is a better way Robert and the only person who can make that happen… is you!"

"Just say what you want me to do?" Robert screamed. "And if you don't. I'll speak to Mum and tell her everything."

The old man sighed loudly. He hadn't expected the boy to be so awkward and cantankerous. The intention had always been for Jack to sit down with Robert and tell him what was required. But things had moved on now, and if he didn't pacify the boy and explain properly what they wanted him to do, Pennington's big secret would be out.

"Alright." Said the old man calmly. "I'll tell you. But if I were you, I'd speak to Jack before anyone else. Do you agree?"

The boy nodded.

"Lots of people have travelled through time Robert." Pennington began cautiously. "Its nothing new. But almost without exception, they've travelled forward in time, exactly like I did, and exactly like Jack did. And the only way to gain access to this new dimension is through a series of subterranean tunnels that appear at certain locations, seemingly at random. And once you've found one, the problem is, you can only travel into the future, and once there, you can never travel back to the present time, or earlier.

It's frightening."

"Go on…" Robert whispered.

"Well." Pennington shrugged his shoulders. "Just think about it. If there was a way to go back in time, you could change things, for the better. And then having travelled back to the present, you could benefit from what you'd done. You could make your life and the lives of those around you, much more comfortable. Would you agree?"

"But…?" Robert interjected. "You already said that it was impossible to travel back into the past. So there's nothing you can do about it?"

"Well up until now." Pennington smiled. "That was the case. But in recent weeks we've found a new portal. Yes its tiny, but the main thing is, it goes back in time, and give or take a few years either way, we know when and where it emerges."

Despite his anger, the boy found it very difficult to hide his obvious curiosity. "Okay." He muttered. "And how can you be so sure?"

"Quite simple really." Pennington announced. "When my cousin Hugh d'Avranches began building Aberlleiniog castle in the year 1080, we had a number of sapling oak trees that were planted only a matter of yards away from the rear wall. And amazingly one of those mighty oak trees still survives. It's at least a hundred feet tall now with an overall girth of thirty-eight feet and six inches, so we know its about nine hundred years old. But if you climb the tree, as I did, only a few days ago, there's something amazing right at the core. In the center of the main trunk, where all the branches head off in their own direction, stretching upwards and outwards towards the light. It's there, at the very heart of the tree. A rippling vacuous space, only large enough for a child to enter, and a direct route to the past, to a place where I Robert Rhuddlan once ruled the whole of North Wales as indisputable lord and master."

"Oh yeah." Said the boy proving yet again how difficult he could be. "And what if you're wrong?"

"No. There's no mistake." Said Pennington confidently. "I put my ear to the void, and what I heard was unmistakable."

Robert just stared at the man.

"It was Hugh himself." Pennington grinned. "My cousin. Hugh The Fat as we always called him, a giant of a man. He was standing somewhere close to the ramparts shouting orders and laughing at the top of his voice. And I have to say… I would recognize that laugh anywhere."

"So." Said Robert angrily. "If you've got such important things to do back in the eleventh century. Why not climb through yourself there and then, and do what you've got to do?"

"I couldn't lad." The old man insisted. "The void itself is very unstable. One wrong move and who knows, it might disappear altogether. Its only big enough for a scrawny youth like you Robert, but not only that, if I had managed to get through, I'd have come face to face with a far more dangerous adversary than cousin Hugh."

Once again Robert just stared at the man open-mouthed.

"Robert of Rhuddlan." Said Pennington. "The butcher!"

If Kathy suspected anything was wrong, she certainly didn't show it. Robert was a bit subdued when they met up again, but as far she could tell, he was just tired. And meanwhile she'd had a lovely time with old Missus Pennington. Ambleside was a beautiful location, the shops were delightful and full of interesting, unusual things, and the weather was glorious. The day had not evolved in the way that Kathy had expected but still, it had been memorable, and inevitably would prove even more eventful.

"Ice-cream anyone?" The old chap smiled. He sounded quite enthusiastic but in truth, was trying hard to conceal his frustration and fatigue. It was a combination of factors. The trek up the Ghyll had not been as leisurely as he remembered and the boy's belligerence, especially for someone so young, had shocked and annoyed him.

"You're spoiling us." Said Kathy. "Why don't I buy the ice-creams instead?"

"Nonsense." Missus Pennington insisted. "I won't hear of it. What would you like Robert...?"

Robert's first impulse was to refuse the offer. He wanted to make it absolutely clear to the old guy that he wouldn't be pushed around. The boy was like his mother, very proud and very stubborn. But the problem was, she was having such a good time and he didn't want to spoil things. And furthermore the "99" cones with a huge serving of vanilla ice-cream, into which a Cadbury's milk chocolate flake had been inserted, looked irresistible. That and the unlikelihood of any nine-year old kid refusing such a treat, unless of course he was sick, which he wasn't, would be very hard to explain.

"I'll have a large cone." Robert smiled rather oddly. "And a flake please... if I may?"

"Of course." Missus Pennington grinned. "That's my boy."

They sat on a low wall close to the Bridge House in the center of town. A curious little dwelling, constructed from local slate in the seventeenth century and a building that had been used by various merchants and artisans over the years. As far as Kathy was concerned a perfect spot to end what she considered a perfect day. They talked again for a while to mister and missus Pennington, before heading back to the Waterhead pier. Kathy thanked them for their kindness and their generosity and Robert did the same, careful to direct his comments to the old lady rather than Pennington himself. It wasn't particularly noticeable but it did provoke a big hug from the woman, which in turn dislodged her hat once again and subsequently made them all laugh.

"Be good Robert" Said Pennington as they waved goodbye. "And always do what your Dad tells you… won't you?"

Robert smiled.

"And don't forget. " Said Missus Pennington. "Its Rose Cottage. Come and see us…please… whenever you like."

Despite summer temperatures, and only a few minutes into the sail, once again Kathy had both hands pushed deep into her pockets and her face turned away from the wind. Robert meanwhile, contrary to earlier in the day, seemed immune to conditions out on the lake, and very preoccupied with his own thoughts. He had a lot on his mind, the least of which was what to think of Pennington's ridiculous story. He felt stupid for even listening to the old man, and wished now that he'd said a lot more.

But before he had chance to mull things over, the two ruffians from Liverpool strode by, looking for an opportunity and chancing their luck.

"Hey kid." The big lad grinned. "Who was that old codger we saw you with?"

"I don't know what you're talking about." Robert answered immediately.

"The old man." Said the scallywag. "Is he your Granddad?"

Robert shot to his feet, but still the boy towered over him. He adjusted his feet until they were slightly further apart than the width of his shoulders. Then raised both hands above chin height, tucked his elbows into his sides, and clenched his fists in readiness.

"No he's bloody well not." Robert growled. "So why don't you get lost, and mind your own business… or else!"

The boys stood their ground, at least for a moment or two. But when they realized the gravity of the situation, the hatred in Robert's eyes, and the fact that he was completely fearless. They skulked away back towards the bow, in search of easier pickings.

"Was that really necessary?" Kathy pleaded. "For goodness sake. I don't know what's got into you at all. All they asked you was… is Mister Pennington your Granddad?"

"Yeah… That's right. " Said Robert sarcastically. "And I gave them my answer."

CHAPTER 7

Kathy looked up at the Town Hall as the coach turned left into Union Street. As she did so, the old clock struck ten. It wasn't dark, not completely anyway, but still, she'd had one heck of a day. Most of the passengers were fast asleep, especially the kids, but not Robert.

And although she would never admit it, she was pleased by the way he'd handled himself on the boat, but was very curious as to why he got so upset.

She decided the best thing to do, was to speak to Jack, and tell him what had happened. He was always sympathetic with the boy and sure to find out what was going on.

And suddenly there he was… waiting for them at the coach terminal.

"Let me guess. You've made us something nice for supper?" Kathy laughed as she stepped off the bus.

"Absolutely." Said Jack as he ruffled up the boy's hair. "I knew you'd be hungry. Especially this one."

"Why. What have you done Dad?" Robert sighed. "You can't cook."

"You'd be surprised what I can do." Jack insisted. "Have you had a good day?"

"Yes. A brilliant day." Kathy smiled. "The best day ever."

"And how about you son?" Said Jack eagerly. "Did you enjoy yourself?"

"It was okay." Said the boy rather reluctantly. "It was different."

"Different?" Kathy shrieked. "Is that the best you can do? Come on Robert. We've had a wonderful time… and you know it?"

"He's probably tired." Said Jack defensively. "So come on. Let's head off and get this supper before it goes cold."

"You've actually made us some supper?" Kathy's eyes opened wide in disbelief.

"Well. Not exactly." Jack had to admit. "But what I have done is persuade the guy at Harper's lane Chippy to stay open till half past ten. So. We better be on our way."

When Jack arrived home from work the following day, the house was empty. Or so it seemed.

In 1955 often as not, people didn't bother to lock their doors. Especially if they'd gone next door to see a neighbor or perhaps a short walk to the shops. So when Jack walked round the back and tried the handle, the door opened immediately and he walked straight in.

A faint smell of toast still lingered in the kitchen, but despite several shouts, no one answered.

When he looked in the pantry, Kathy's shopping basket was still there, suggesting she hadn't gone far. So before she came back, the obvious thing to do was make a cup of tea.

And if…when they'd first moved in, all those years ago, Jack could have afforded a thicker carpet and better underlay? Who knows? He might never have heard the floorboards creaking. But he did, and suddenly it dawned on him, there might be someone in the house after all.

He waited momentarily for the water to boil, and when the kettle screamed, he ignored it completely and very stealthily, he crept upstairs.

There were two bedrooms on the back of the house. One they'd always referred to as the spare room, the other was Roberts, and both doors were slightly ajar. It seemed obvious to try the boy's room first, but when he looked inside, it was empty, and when he tried the spare room, exactly the same. He dashed across the landing and in quick succession, searched his and Kathy's room and the bathroom, all to no avail.

The house was empty.

But when he walked into Robert's bedroom for a second time and looked through the back bedroom window, he could see the boy, curled up on a deckchair at the bottom of the garden.

"Hey… What are you up to?" Jack sighed as he stepped out onto the lawn.

Robert didn't flinch. He had his head in a book, and as Jack got closer, he knew exactly what the boy was reading.

"I bought that book." Said Jack rather warily.

Robert still didn't speak.

"An interesting subject… don't you think?" Jack smiled ruefully.

"Yeah. I guess so." The boy agreed. "So… when did you buy it?"

"A few years ago." Said Jack. "I was a bit older than what you are now."

"And what do you reckon?" Robert demanded to know. "About H.G. Wells and his Time Machine, is it any good?"

"It depends what you're looking for." Said Jack. "If it's just a bit of entertainment you're after, it's fine. But I suspect not. Am I right?"

"Well the thing is Dad." Robert growled. "We met this old man yesterday up in the Lakes. He knew all about you. He said he knew where you lived, what you did for a job and more importantly… he knew where you came from. And what this chap didn't know about time travel… wasn't worth knowing?"

"If you don't mind lad?" Jack insisted. "I'd like to finish this conversation indoors… please."

Jack stormed off back towards the house, and eventually the boy followed. They sat down directly across from each other at the kitchen table, and for what seemed like an eternity, neither of them spoke.

"Okay." Jack muttered at long last. "So you met this chap…?"

"Pennington!" Said the boy at a stroke. "That's his name."

"Yes." Said Jack softly. "And did you like the man?"

"No." Said Robert. "Why should I?"

"That's not what your Mum said."

"No maybe not." The boy insisted. "But she didn't have to listen to all that rubbish that came out of his mouth, did she?"

"That sounds a bit harsh." Jack sighed. "Was it really that bad?"

"The man's a liar!" The boy fumed. "And I don't trust him."

Jack stared at the boy, both eyebrows raised. "Can we discuss it?" He whispered.

Robert shrugged.

"Alright." Jack conceded. "You're upset, I understand. I should have spoken to you, before you went up to the Lakes. So I made a mistake? And the old man… he just wanted to meet you, and find out what sort of lad you were, and I agreed."

"Why?" Robert snarled. "What's it got to do with him?"

"Because…" Said Jack. "Because he's family."

"No he's not." The boy insisted. "He's just a stupid old man."

"He's your Granddad Robert." Jack sighed. "That's who he is."

Slowly but surely, the boy's face, already pink with rage, resigned itself entirely to one of disbelief. Jack could see his pain and wanted to help, but chose instead to say nothing, allowing his son enough time to blink back the tears.

"Why should I believe you?" Robert sniffed.

"Because its true." Jack groaned. "I swear."

"Everything else?" The boy pleaded. "Is that true as well?"

Jack nodded.

"And all that stuff about you and him travelling through time." Robert shouted. "That actually happened?"

"I'm afraid so." Said Jack.

Until that moment, Robert would never have dared to speak out against his father, but Jack's attitude was pitiful, and the boy needed answers. Kathy had always told him to stand up for himself and to never let anyone keep him under. "Don't live in the shadows" She insisted. "And make sure you get what you want."

And that's exactly what the boy intended to do. From now on, he would respond to situations rather than react, and despite how others might behave, he would always keep control of his emotions and be true to himself.

When he spoke again there was no heat in his voice, the earlier tension was gone and his young lips bore the semblance of a smile.

"Let's start at the beginning. Shall we?" Said Robert calmly. "And tell me what you remember?"

Jack was lost in thought. "There's not much I do remember." He mumbled. "Although I do have a strange recollection about Aberlleiniog, and the first time I went back there, it all seemed very familiar."

"What year was that?" Asked the boy.

"Early 1930's." Jack sighed. "Gerald took me down there."

"And had you met Pennington then, at that stage?" Robert asked.

"No. I met him for the first time in 1939, just before the war." Jack insisted. "Gerald introduced us."

"So. He didn't waste any time getting reacquainted did he?" Said Robert sarcastically. "About twenty years?"

"He had no idea that we'd followed him through the void." Said Jack. "As far as he was aware, we'd died nine hundred years ago."

"So how did Gerald find him?"

"He did what you did yesterday." Jack insisted. "Had a day in the Lakes. Called at the local butchers in Ambleside, and low and behold, there he was. Standing behind the counter in his bloodstained apron, a sharp knife in hand, and the proceeds of his handiwork hanging down all around him. Old habits die hard, at least that's what Gerald said."

"And what was Gerald's reaction?"

"Shocked to say the least." Said Jack. "But what you must never forget is that these two men are brothers, and back in the eleventh century, Gerald swore an oath of allegiance to his brother. A lifetime obligation to support and defend him and even now nine hundred years later, he still obeys him."

"And when you met Pennington?" Said Robert. "What did you think of the man?"

"He can be very likeable." Jack winced. "But then again, he's a complicated man. And… like it or it. He is my father."

"So why didn't you tell Mum?" Robert's eyes opened wide. "And Missus Pennington. Surely they had a right to know?"

"Your Granddad… your real Granddad that is." Jack sighed. "He forbade it. He always said the fewer people who knew the better, and insisted that if you told them, most of them would never believe you. He was right of course. People can be quite gullible, but the minute you tell them you're a time traveller, they think you've gone soft in the head."

"What's changed now then?" Said the boy calmly. "And why should I be any different? Either you and the old man have gone completely bonkers or there's something back in the eleventh century that you two can't wait to get your hands. So which is?"

"I've never seen it obviously." Jack stressed. "But he has explained it to me, and from what I can gather, I can't emphasize enough how significant this thing is."

"Let me guess." Said the boy sarcastically. "Some loot he's stolen all those years ago. Gold, diamonds, I don't know, whatever…"

"No. It's not treasure." Jack insisted. "Not like we would imagine anyway. What Robert of Rhuddlan acquired nine hundred years ago, is very special. An item of antiquity, just as important now as it was all those years ago, a manuscript with lavish decorations and instructions of huge potential. Originally it was part of the Book of Kells and what is often described as the missing pages from the Gospel of Saint John."

Robert's nose twitched with derision. "If you think that I'm going to crawl down some god-forsaken hole in the center of an old oak tree." He growled. "In order to get my hands on a lousy book...you've got another thing coming."

"Well son. At the end of the day, that will be your decision." Jack insisted. "But that lousy book, as you put it, is the most important source of information, that anyone could ever lay their hands on."

It would take more than a few strong words to impress the boy, especially now. All along he'd held the view that what they wanted him to retrieve, was some huge stash of druid gold. Either that or a chest full of silver coins they'd stolen from the Welsh princes. The whole story of course was completely ridiculous from start to finish, and as far as Robert was concerned, they could get someone else. He pushed his chair back and moved away from the table as Kathy walked in from the lounge.

Jack's explanation was already at an end, but still, the swiftness of Kathy's arrival had evidently unnerved him.

"I thought you were out." He stuttered.

"I was." She said abruptly. "But now I'm back. So. What have I missed?"

Jack's response was hardly convincing, but then again, neither was the boy's. As Kathy looked on, both of them shook their heads in unison. The meeting may have ended in stalemate, but despite their disagreement, they recognized the importance of keeping quiet.

"Good." Said Kathy. "That's what I like. A nice happy home to come back to."

CHAPTER 8

Spending four weeks with Grandpa Gerald in Wales was something that Robert had considered very carefully. When Kathy first told the boy what she was planning, he wasn't that keen, but gradually, he'd changed his mind. He'd no intention of doing anything he didn't want, but this was a chance to get away and an opportunity too good to miss. Kathy dragged the suitcase from under the bed and began to pack his things. It was old and battered and suitably small, handy for the boy to manage all by himself and in truth quite convenient. But it wasn't long before every inch of available space had been crammed, with little room for anything else, and in particular the H.G. Wells novel.

"I want that." Robert insisted. "To read on the train."

"Take a comic instead." Kathy suggested. "You've enough to carry."

"Maybe." Said Robert tenaciously. "But the thing is, I've already started it."

"Well that's up to you." Kathy sighed obediently. "You decide."

She stopped what she was doing, ran her fingers through the boy's inky black curls and kissed him gently on the top of his head.

"I'll leave it to you." She insisted. "You know what you're doing."

And she was right. Robert had a plan and immediately his mum left the room he reached into his pocket and pulled out a substantial piece of paper, unfolded it carefully, and once again examined it, in every single detail. He'd taken it from an old handbag in Kathy's wardrobe, where she kept all the families important documents. She had no idea that the boy had seized it, but as far as Robert was concerned, it was his, and his alone. And if there was one thing that no one could ever dispute. It was the ownership of an individual's birth certificate, a certified copy, pursuant to the Births and Deaths Registration Act of 1874. An interesting record that the boy had seen before but never really studied. And the one thing that stood out above anything else was Jack Rudd's details. Under the column for rank or profession of father, it did state Jack's trade very clearly, but after the word "Electrician" it also said in brackets… (Journeyman).

The word itself captured the attention of a nine-year old boy with big ambitions and an even bigger imagination. And not only that, it also helped him to picture the early events in Jack Rudd's troubled life. From the moment that Jack had been carried into the void by Grandpa Gerald in the eleventh century, to the point where the child had re-emerged nine hundred years later. Still in mortal danger from those that might pursue him and ultimately destroy him, but like Robert of Rhuddlan himself an adventurer and journeyman leaping from one period in time to another, in order to escape and ultimately change his destiny.

And then, from a second pocket Robert pulled out yet another piece of paper, and in exactly the same manner unfolded it and laid it on the bed to scrutinize his prize. He took no pride in what he'd done, but once again, he'd got what he wanted. A visit to the reference section of Chorley Library earlier in the day had enabled him to tear an individual page from a beautiful leather bound book on British Castles and Fortifications. It was simply a case of necessity and the only way he could get his hands on an A4 coloured photograph of Skipton Castle was to become a literary vandal.

Robert unfastened the suitcase for a second time, and very carefully he concealed the birth certificate, the photograph and his treasured penknife in among his clothes, away from prying eyes.

The following morning it was all go.

Jack came in to see the boy, but didn't have long, and the clock was ticking. He hugged Robert very quickly, told him to be a good lad for Grandpa Gerald and rushed off to work.

Robert wished he hadn't bothered, and Jack wished he'd said a few more things, whilst he still had the chance.

"Come on Robert." Kathy shouted loudly. "You need to eat. You've a long busy day ahead of you."

The boy staggered downstairs as fast as he could paying little attention to anything, but then suddenly, as he reached the bottom step, was obliged to step over a much larger suitcase, propped up against the wall alongside his own. Robert stopped for a moment to think, and the only obvious thing he could imagine, was that they wanted him to take yet another case full of stuff for Grandpa Gerald?

He grabbed hold of it to see how heavy it was, and even though he could just about lift it, made his mind up straight away… this second piece of luggage was staying in Lancashire.

"You need to get your skates on." Kathy insisted as the boy stepped into the kitchen. "We've only got half an hour, before the taxi arrives."

Robert's train would leave Wigan at ten past nine and if everything went according to plan, he'd be in Crewe before eleven o' clock. He'd have to wait in Crewe for an hour and then catch the connection to Bangor in North Wales. With a bit of luck, Grandpa Gerald would be able to pick him up from Bangor station about three o' clock and drive them back to his little cottage in Anglesey, on the edge of Llangoed village. It was quite an adventure, but something that the boy was looking forward to, as soon as he'd wiped the sleep from his eyes.

Robert slumped down on the chair and proceeded to drown his cornflakes in a deluge of unpasteurized milk.

"Will the taxi be expensive mum?" Robert asked between mouthfuls.

"I don't know yet." Said Kathy. "We'll have to wait and see?"

"And what happens at Wigan station?" He continued. "Are you going to see me off?"

"Don't worry." Said Kathy. "Its all taken care of."

"I'm not worried." Said the boy confidently. "I just wanted to know if the taxi was going to wait for you, and bring you back home… that's all?"

Kathy smiled.

"And that other suitcase?" Robert insisted. "I hope that's not for me?"

"No. It's not." Said Kathy hurriedly. "So come on, stop talking and hurry up."

Seemingly somewhat distracted by the boy's comments, she sat down at the far end of the table and began scribbling on a piece of paper. Robert tried to see what she was writing, but Kathy cupped her left arm around the note, exactly like he did at school, when the next kid along, would try to copy his work. It wasn't a long letter that's for sure and only took her a few minutes. And as soon she'd signed it, it was folded, whisked away into an envelope and sealed.

Breakfast over, Kathy washed all the pots and tidied up immediately, and as she brushed her hair in the mirror, suddenly Robert became very conscious of how pretty his mum really was. When she was young Kathy had always despised what everyone described as her mousy colored hair, but now the short no-nonsense hairstyle brought warmth to her features. It was a simple look and like the color of an oak tree, not too dark, appeared quite gentle in any light, and a perfect contrast to the black knee length skirt and noticeably tight fitting teal coloured sweater.

The young woman always looked smart, but today was particularly fetching.

When the taxi arrived they were just about ready, and as Kathy locked the back door and walked through the house, the last thing she did was to pick up the envelope and leave it in a prominent position at the side of the cooker. Until that moment Robert hadn't realized she'd written Jack's name on it, but now he knew. And as far as he was concerned, that could mean only one thing. Kathy was going with him.

The taxi driver was an old guy with the widest shoulders that Robert had ever seen, even broader than those of John Bingham the butcher, and his were quite magnificent. Although on closer inspection, this guy was somewhat hunched, and when the boy studied the man more carefully, his withered old face and fringe of grey-white hair, there was no comparison, to the man who'd spent the best part of his life behind the knife.

"Just these two missus?" The man growled as he pointed to the suitcases in the hallway."

"Yes thank you." Said Kathy politely. "That's all."

The man's face seemed to crumple as he picked up the larger of the two pieces of luggage and suddenly he didn't look quite as powerful.

Robert and his mum climbed into the back of the old Humber Snipe, and a few minutes later they were off.

When the steam train left Glasgow at six, her water tanks were full to overflowing. Three hours later at Wigan North West, the beast had guzzled five thousand gallons of water already, and craved for more. She pulled into the station in her usual belligerent way, like a giant rhino from the African plains. Unashamedly dirty, noisy and seemingly always quarrelsome. Her metal wheels, gears and bars were covered in oil and grease but despite the filth, she never disappointed.

As she came to a halt at the platform, and the passengers rushed forward to climb on board, her huge robust cylindrical body still belched and clanked with stubborn disobedience.

The intrepid duo joined the bun fight like everyone else until eventually they gained access to the corridor walkway that extended the full length of their carriage. And all they had to do then, was find an empty seating compartment, drag their luggage inside, and make it their own.

Robert spread himself out on the bench seat across from Kathy and stared out at the passengers, waiting patiently on platform five.

"They're going north mum." He said. "Up to the Lakes."

"Yeah, I guess so." Said Kathy. "And we've done that already. So now son… its time for something new."

Robert put both thumbs up. "It'll be fun."

"It will." Said Kathy. Although I'm not quite sure that Grandpa Gerald will agree?"

"Does he know you're coming?" The boy gasped.

Kathy shook her head.

"No. I'm afraid not. She sighed. "Grandpa's arranged to pick you up from Bangor railway station at three o' clock, but as far as he knows, you're coming by yourself."

"Will he be mad?" Robert asked mischievously.

"I'm not sure." Kathy smirked. "That's up to him isn't it? You know what he's like?"

"You could have phoned him?" Robert insisted. "He's got a telephone."

"That's true." Kathy nodded. "But I'd made my mind up anyway. So there was no point. And we haven't got a phone have we? Anyway that's my excuse."

"And Dad." Robert gulped. "What did he say?"

"By the time your Dad finds out, we'll be there already." Kathy grinned. "He won't see my letter until he gets home."

"And what about the job?" Said Robert. "I thought you had to work this week?"

"I went to see Mister Burton a few days ago." She smiled. "Before I bought myself a ticket. I explained it was a family matter and I had to go away for a few days to help out, and he was okay with that. He was really nice actually. He said come back when you're ready and the job would still be there."

Robert always knew that his mum was a bit of a schemer, but now as far as the boy was concerned, she'd earned herself a few more brownie points. He stared in awe at the young woman, wondering how someone so plain and unassuming could be so devilishly cunning.

Suddenly the guard waved his green flag and the whistle blew. A group of spectators stepped back away from the beast and the train began to shudder. A copious amount of oil had obviously splashed onto the track and as the engineer applied a bit too much power, the huge wheels started to spin. Wheel slip was a particular problem with some of the larger steam engines, but the stoker had a solution. He jumped off the footplate with a spade in hand, and made his way to the sandbox. And a few minutes later, having covered the track with shovelfuls of the stuff, he climbed back on board and the driver tried again. The second attempt was much more successful and to everyone's relief, the giant loco began to move very, very slowly away from the station and gathered speed. And what was left behind was a narrow piece of ground now covered in golden sand, and the nearest thing the town of Wigan would ever get to its own beach.

"And before you ask." Kathy laughed. "I think Grandpa Gerald only has one spare bed and therefore the answer is yes…you will have to sleep with me."

The boy grimaced as if what he'd heard was the worst news ever, but actually, he didn't mind at all.

CHAPTER 9

Like any other nine year old, Robert was thrilled at the prospect of a proper summer holiday at last, and soaked up the views from the window as the train began its journey. Predictably the landscape between Wigan and Warrington was very industrial and at times quite bleak, but once they'd left Warrington Bank Quay and headed south, the terrain changed dramatically. It was a lot more pleasing to the eye. Open green fields and rolling countryside, littered by tiny lanes and numerous ancient canals that crisscrossed many areas of the north west of England.

At long last they reached Crewe. A railway station blanketed in soot, and after a hundred and thirty years of steam, with passenger and freight trains, passing through this major junction on the West coast main line. It was hard to find a section of the huge glass roof or a cast iron column that wasn't sullied by smoke. An hour's wait was just about bearable until eventually, the Holyhead train arrived, and soon they were on their way. Fortunate once again to have a compartment all to them selves, Kathy and the boy had few distractions, and all that was left to do, was sit back, relax and enjoy the views.

The locomotive pressed on quickly towards Chester and immediately the scenery improved. A profusion of brilliant green pastures, many of them dotted with shaggy sheep and an amazing abundance of wild flowers. It was a landscape of warm summer colors, but in the distance, much further to the west, a suggestion of larger hills. Each one of them flushed with pinks and purples and covered completely in huge swathes of heather.

Robert pretended to himself that this was 1840 and the train that he was on, was heading through the badlands in South Dakota, and if they made it through to Bangor, he wondered if they'd ever make it back. And he wasn't even sure that he wanted to.

After Chester it was off to the coast, to Shotton, Flint and Prestatyn. A coastline littered with beaches. On the left hand side of the track were cattle grazing on the lower slopes, on the right a few small boats bobbing about in the water, tugging against their anchor chains as the tide came rushing in. And inlets where the water lay more still and offered up a silvery sheen, reflecting back towards the land.

The boy had intended to read his book on the journey, but the journey itself was too good to miss. He'd thought long and hard about what could happen, should he chose to visit Aberlleiniog, and if he did, confident he had a plan. And a sudden glow of pleasure came over him, excited at the prospect that if it succeeded, it might make him rich.

"Look." Said Kathy. "It's a castle."

And sure enough there was Gwrych castle in the distance, a huge fortified building on the outskirts of Abergele, a magical place, shimmering in the sunlight, large cliffs to the rear, stunning views out towards the coast.

"Wow." The boy shouted. "Its magnificent."

And so it was.

Robert dashed into the corridor, opened the nearest drop light window, and locked the leather strap in place. Fascinated by the sight he leaned out, and very soon, along with many others who'd done exactly the same thing, came vaguely aware of the smoke from the engine as it snaked along at the side of the train. Sooty smog from the partly burnt coal that stung his eyes and blackened his face. As the castle disappeared behind them, the boy dragged him-self back inside. And as he turned to face her, Kathy's grin got wider.

"What are you like?" She sighed. "Listen son, you need to take a look in the mirror."

"I haven't got a mirror." The boy complained. "Can I borrow yours?"

"Come over here." Kathy insisted as she licked her handkerchief. "Grandpa Gerald won't recognize you. You look like a chimney sweep."

The boy laughed.

And therefore when the massive round towers of Conway castle came into view, Robert decided to stay put and enjoy the sights from the comfort of their compartment. Built on the Eastern side of the River Conway in 1283, it took a huge work force less than ten years to complete, but the end result was spectacular. Dominating the estuary completely, it was one of the finest examples of late thirteenth century military architecture. Robert had seen pictures of Conway, on the day he scoured Chorley library for a photograph of Skipton castle, yet nothing could have prepared him for the breathtaking views that he now enjoyed.

He wondered if Aberlleiniog was anything like as grand. He didn't think so, but now he'd seen Conway castle, it was inevitable... he would have to find out?

After all, from what the boy had learned, both castles had been built for the very same reason. Give or take two hundred years, it was the same objective. Conquer the Welsh princes, take their lands and crush them completely. Although as Robert of Rhuddlan had discovered, there was always a price to pay.

The last leg of the journey was Conway to Bangor and undoubtedly the most exciting. As the old steam train raced on using a line that for the greater part of its route, had been carved out of the coastal cliffs. It offered an amazing panorama on one side down to the Irish Sea, and on the other, a view of the huge mountains on the edge of Snowdonia.

These were rocky escarpments and rugged peaks, bisected time and again by trickling streams and what could only be described as single trails. Many of them hardly used by humans but for most of the year, would be littered with thousands of tiny sheep droppings and rabbit poo. It was a beautiful place to walk and explore but each season would present it's own challenges. In summer there was a constant threat of fires up on the moors, in autumn and winter, biting winds and danger from exposure. And in the spring as the snow began to melt, almost overnight, those same tiny streams would transform into tumbling waterfalls that plummeted down the mountain. Hurtling beneath the railway along huge storm drain's that safeguarded the integrity of the track.

The train stopped twice on this particular section, once at Penmaenmawr and then again at Llanfairfechan, both villages renown for their spectacular mountain views and coastal walks. And then finally, at long last… at least for Kathy and the boy, the final destination… Bangor.

Bangor was the last mainland station on the North Wales coastline between Crewe and Holyhead, a busy station in terms of passenger numbers and a hub that served the surrounding community, south towards Caernarfon, and even further afield.

When they stepped off the train and looked around for Grandpa Gerald, he was nowhere to be seen. But then suddenly as the influx of new passengers made their way along the platform towards the barrier, they saw him standing in the shade. He looked weary, mean and cranky. And despite a few years younger than his eminently more notorious brother, he looked a lot older. As he propped him self up with a walking cane, and peered out from under his sun hat, his bristled chin emerged from out of the shadows, white with whiskers.

"Hello Gerald." Said Kathy as she walked towards him. "And how are you?"

Gerald's eyes flashed brightly, an expression of frustration etched across his face, like a man who had long since forgotten what it felt like, to have joints that moved freely, without pain. And a man with a story to tell, although often as not, would prefer to remain silent.

"I'm alright love." He gasped. "This is a surprise."

"I know." Kathy smiled. "I got an few extra days holiday, and I didn't want to waste it."

Gerald frowned in disbelief, his big blue eyes bore right through her, an intense penetrating stare that Kathy was strong enough to resist, a response that the old man had obviously not expected. Eventually he looked away and ruffled the boy's hair with his stubby old fingers.

"And how are you little one?" He growled. "Are you behaving yourself?"

Robert had always wondered why most adults thought it was funny when they messed with your hair. He'd got used it. It was what men did, especially the older ones. But he did take umbrage if anyone suggested that he was small for his age.

"Always." He answered defiantly. "But us little ones can do things that you old ones can't."

"Ooh. Is that so?" The old man groaned. "I better be careful with you lad. I may have hit a nerve?"

"Robert. Say sorry to your Grandpa." Kathy demanded. "He's only having a bit of fun that's all. "Isn't that right Gerald?"

"Absolutely." The old man roared with laughter. "And I have to agree son. There are definitely things that you young ones can do, that us old ones can't."

"Sorry Grandpa." Robert grinned. "I'm a bit tired."

"Apology accepted." Gerald insisted. "But meanwhile, I'm very impressed, and I can't imagine for one minute, that you're frightened of anyone."

"I'm not." Said Robert loudly. "And the bigger they come, the harder they fall."

"Well I never… young Master Rudd." Said the old man. "Now you've got me thinking, and I'm beginning to wonder whom on earth you might take after?"

Gerald's shiny black car was one of the cheapest but most reliable vehicles on the British market, a four-door saloon with a huge headlight on top of each wing and indicators that would spring out from the door pillars. An old Ford Prefect that had more than enough boot space to accommodate both suitcases, and leather upholstery, which gave it a bit of class. As Kathy climbed up front with Grandpa Gerald, Robert spread himself out across the whole rear seat in his usual manner. And if there was one thing the boy did recognize, it was the smell of opulence and the feel of animal skin as it rubbed against his flesh. Something he'd always enjoyed, even as an infant. But when the vehicle had been sitting in the sun for an hour or two, as Grandpa Gerald's had, and all the boy was wearing was a pair of knee pants and a short-sleeved shirt, it was a painful experience.

"Wind all the windows down, as fast as you can." The old man insisted. "And lets get going."

The vehicle lurched forward immediately onto the roadway, then headed off towards Telford's bridge, and the island of Anglesey.

Before 1826 there was no bridge, so when Robert of Rhuddlan was Lord of all North Wales, often as not, he would cross the Menai Strait by ferry, a perilous journey, over fast flowing and dangerous waters. Where farmers would drive their cattle across to the opposite shore, forcing them to swim, a cruel but unavoidable practice that led to the death of many valuable beasts. By 1955 however, those days were long gone, and mercifully all the animals would make it to market. The Menai Strait was no less dangerous, but at least now, there were two bridges, one for road traffic and one for rail.

And as they left the mainland behind and headed off along the coast towards Beaumaris, it seemed to Robert, like he was going home. It was all very strange, and despite having never been to the island, he had a weird sense of recollection. Apart from a day in the Lake District, he'd never seen such incredible countryside, and once again the views were spectacular. The road north from Menai Bridge was a challenging drive, even more so in the winter, with regular road closures, often due to falling trees and rock- falls. And in the strait itself, where surging tides converge from opposite directions, frequent incidents of boats capsizing or foundering on the rocks. A wild, exciting place where a fit young lad like Robert Rudd would either grow up very quickly, given half the chance, or get himself killed in the process.

"Did you see Conway Castle lad?" Grandpa Gerald exhaled sharply. "From the train?"

"Yeah I did Grandpa." Said the boy.

The old man gazed up at the rear-view mirror.

"And what did you think son?" He asked. "Impressive eh?"

"The biggest castle I've ever seen." Robert nodded. "It was huge."

"Well. Keep looking." Grandpa Gerald insisted. "You've got another treat in store."

And as the road widened, and they drove along beside the boat yard at Gallows Point, the town of Beaumaris came into view, a delightful seaside resort, with a mix of medieval, Georgian, Victorian and Edwardian architecture. Considered by many, to be Anglesey's jewel in the crown, a site chosen by Edward The First, for the last of his "Iron Ring Of Castles". It was yet another symbol of "Longshanks" obsession, and his desperate attempt, to control the Welsh.

And the castle was amazing.

After numerous revolts and skirmishes, work had begun in 1295, on what was intended to be the most perfect example of symmetrical concentric planning. A castle, that had it ever been completed, would have closely resembled Harlech castle. It was surrounded by a huge moat and tidal dock, allowing the castle to be supplied directly from the sea, but sadly by 1330 the building work had ceased.

Grandpa Gerald pulled up alongside to give them both a better view. And as Robert hung out of the car window, his eyes twinkled with excitement, mesmerized by the light and the colors. The boy had an irresistible urge to smile, knowing all too well, that if only he were brave enough, he might go back to a juncture in time, before any of this existed. To a point in antiquity when the only medieval castle to dominate this particular coastline, was owned by his ancestor. This was Robert of Rhuddlan's territory long before Edward Longshanks came on the throne. And if he could rule the Welsh, as Robert obviously did, until that fateful day when he stepped into the void, then so could Robert Rudd.

The boy's plan was simple. He'd go back in time, secure his relationship with Robert of Rhuddlan. Get Robert's army to swear an allegiance to him, as Robert's natural successor. And when the time came for his Grandfather to travel on into the future, as he must. It was then, that Robert Rudd, the boy king, would defeat the Welsh rebels, once and for all.

Robert Rudd had no intention of going back to those "dark satanic mills" of the industrial north. He'd been to the Lake District and seen for himself what England's green and pleasant land could look like. And as he looked across at the shimmering strait, the beauty of the mountains in the distance, and the peaceful meadows all around him, he realized why this was a land worth fighting for. He wasn't interested in any lousy book that his father had asked him to get his hands on. As far as the boy was concerned, if Robert of Rhuddlan really was a butcher, then so be it. He would be the butcher's boy. And the only question he couldn't answer was… what would happen to Kathy, if he never returned?

CHAPTER 10

It was a fifteen-minute drive to Grandpa Gerald's place in Llangoed. A tiny property, but like a lot of others in this part of Wales, an old stone cottage built of big rough boulders and roofed with slate from a nearby mountain quarry. Many of the stones, especially those at ground level were covered in moss and at the front of the house, an old wooden door, the likes of which would be hard to find outside the pages of a Nordic fairytale. Positioned on the outskirts of the village, the old man could come and go as he pleased, with no one else the wiser, and that suited him down to the ground. It was an area covered by mature predominately broadleaf woodland, extending down towards the coast and to the very fringes of the Menai Strait. When he purchased the house many years ago at the request of others, he'd accepted the burden that went with ownership. It was a difficult undertaking even then, but as the years crept by, things got even harder. For the time being however, this was still the house of the Gatekeeper, and as the boy would soon learn, the present incumbent took his responsibilities very seriously.

"So. This is it." Gerald sighed loudly as he scrambled out of the vehicle, his shirt soaked with sweat. "If you come inside, I'll show you around. But trust me, it won't take long."

Kathy was glad she'd made the journey, but with thoughts of spending time indoors, with a grumpy old man and temperatures in the eighties, she gazed across at the cottage with some trepidation, and wondered what the boy was thinking.

She needn't have worried, the kid was more resilient than she knew, and anyway within a few hours, things would be different. The cottage was incredibly cosy but surprisingly cool and despite having to share a bed, as Kathy had predicted, it wasn't as crowded as what she first thought.

As long as Kathy had known Grandpa Gerald he'd lived alone, and that was that. Neither he nor Jack would ever speak about the past, and always avoided any mention of Grandma Rudd. Kathy assumed the woman had walked, but nagging doubts had always remained. Each time she'd broached the subject with Jack and insisted the boy had a right to know who his Grandma was, Jack would clam up and refuse to talk. He should have told Kathy everything when they first married, but the longer it went on, the harder it became, until eventually impossible to discuss. And the truth was, Gerald never had a partner, and sadly because Robert's Grandma didn't make it through the void, the boy would never meet her. Not in normal circumstances anyway. But if Pennington was right, and if Robert could travel back in time, it might just happen.

And so, after forty years on the edge of isolation, Gerald's little cottage bore no indication of a woman's touch. The ultimate man cave, devoid of femininity, deprived of color, and decades since a female footstep had echoed within its walls. A little musty but nothing that opening a few windows and doors, couldn't solve. And despite a few angry stares from the old man, Kathy drew back the curtains in every room. The house needed light, and as far as she was concerned, it couldn't come soon enough.

She rummaged through the kitchen cupboards and wondered how Grandpa Gerald coped in normal circumstances. With hardly enough food for one, she would have to go to the village.

"Is it far Gerald?" Kathy questioned the old man. "To the shops?"

"About ten minutes on foot." He answered gruffly. "Why what do you need?"

"Well. Let me see now." Said Kathy somewhat disparagingly. "How about we buy some food, what do you think. Is that a good idea?"

Gerald's stare narrowed and once again he appeared to judge her, precisely as he'd done a little earlier back at the station. And whether she was genuinely hurt by his response, it didn't seem to matter. When Kathy's eyes flashed with anger and indignation, exactly as before, he felt compelled to back away.

"Yeah. You're probably right." He mumbled. "We do need a few things. Here take this."

And before the young woman had time to say another word, he'd stuffed a fistful of bank notes into her hand, and stepped outside.

"I'll come with you mum." Said the boy eagerly.

"No. Stay here with old grumpy." Kathy insisted. "And for God's sake lad. Please. Try and put a smile on his face will you?"

Kathy grabbed some bags from the pantry and set off immediately. She'd only taken a few steps however, when the old man shouted after her.

"Don't forget Kathy." They speak Welsh here." He insisted. "So when you're in the shop, don't be surprised if you're the only one speaking English. And if you think they're talking about you behind your back. You're probably right. Oh yeah…I almost forgot, we need some potatoes."

Kathy ignored him and carried on walking, and he wondered for a while if she'd heard him. But whether she had or whether she hadn't, he didn't shout again.

And as soon as she'd gone, Gerald slumped down on a rickety old bench at the front of the house. "Come over here son." He insisted. "We need to talk you and I."

Robert strode up to Grandpa Gerald as if he meant business. His emotions were under control, but there was anger boiling up inside. He hated how the old man had spoken to Kathy but realized any irritation he was feeling, would have to be contained. The boy ran a hand through his hair several times in quick succession and fixed the man with a stare so severe, his eyes looked like they might pop out at any minute. It was a skill he'd inherited from his mother and a look that could stop a grizzly in its tracks.

"I understand, you're angry." The old man growled. "Its not what you expected is it? But if you think about it, there's not a lot I can do to change things."

"You could be nicer." Said the boy.

"Yeah well. Maybe your right?" Said Grandpa Gerald. "But when you've lived on your own for a long time, its not easy."

"No. Obviously not." Robert nodded. "So. What do you want to talk about?"

"Straight to the point. I like that." The old man grinned. "It runs in the family."

The boy didn't answer.

"I just wanted a chat. That's all." Said Gerald. "And then you know."

"About what?" The boy frowned.

"About the void." The old man whispered. "From what I can gather you've heard all about it."

"I've heard some ridiculous story, if that's what you mean." Said Robert. "From yet another old man, who reckons he's my real Granddad."

"I know." Said Gerald brusquely. "It's confusing."

"No its not" The boy pleaded. "It's just a load of rubbish…that's all? "

The old man stared dead ahead.

"Unfortunately not." Said Gerald eventually. "I wish it was, but for what's it worth. If I was your real Grandpa, you would never have found out."

Robert listened carefully.

"I would never have told you." Gerald insisted. "What my brother is asking you to do is fraught with danger, and you must be aware of that."

"My dad had no objections to me coming here?" The boy interjected. "In fact, just the opposite. He encouraged it?"

"Yes I know." Said Gerald disapprovingly. "And I won't defend him. But what I do understand is how Jack has been manipulated by your Granddad and the influence that Robert of Rhuddlan can exercise over anyone with whom he comes into contact." Gerald sighed loudly. "And I consider myself a prime example. Although of late… I have begun to question some of the things he's asked me to do?"

"He's got no control over me." Said Robert.

"That's easy said." Insisted Gerald. "But the man is used to getting his own way."

"Okay then." The hint of a cunning smile inched its way across the boy's face. "You better tell me everything. We mustn't disappoint him."

Kathy's prolonged absence from the cottage was a good opportunity for Gerald and the youngster to talk, but before too long, they could see her walking back along the lane, her long skinny arms straining by her sides with the weight of the shopping, her face uncomfortably flushed and clammy.

"I think she's struggling." Said Robert intuitively as he got to his feet. "We best go and help her."

The sun went down slowly that evening, and when it did, even young Robert would notice how dark it could be in an area of the country so sparsely inhabited by people. Back in Lancashire the night sky was never this black, but not only that, he'd never seen such a huge number of stars that stretched away into distance, and only the occasional bark from a faraway hound, disturbed the silence of the night.

And once in bed he snuggled up to Kathy, hoping desperately for a cuddle. And sure enough she did just that, cradling the boy's head against her breast, meddling playfully as she tugged the inky black curls between her fingers.

She loved the boy. She loved him more than anyone, including Jack, and more than anyone could possibly imagine. He infuriated her almost every single day, especially with that damned stupid football and stroppy attitude, but despite all that, she wouldn't change him for the world.

She was there for a reason, and whatever it took to keep her boy safe, Kathy would do it, without question.

Within a few minutes the boy was unconscious, and for him, the night would be an opportunity for eight hours of uninterrupted sleep. For Kathy however, it wasn't so, and at two in the morning, still wide-awake, she recognized the sound of footsteps shuffling by in the corridor outside their bedroom. Grandpa Gerald was trying to be quiet, but completely unaware of how his own hearing had deteriorated over the last few years, he never realised that Kathy's was razor sharp and because of that, she would hear everything.

She slipped out of bed, careful not to disturb the boy, and when she sensed the coast was clear, lifted the latch on the bedroom door and like a thief slinking about in the shadows, edged her way barefoot along the passage towards the snug.

Breathing slowly through her nose, and mindful of tripping up in the darkness, she tiptoed on, placing the ball of each foot down carefully, shifting her weight very gently to one foot and then the other, until eventually she reached the door to Gerald's hidey hole.

Suddenly a chink of light appeared in the tiny space around the doorframe, and a moment later, the pulsating sound of an old rotary telephone pierced the silence, when Grandpa Gerald's big fat fingers began to dial.

And a few seconds later, when he'd dialed the last digit, Kathy could hear the telephone ringing very,

very faintly at the other end of the line. She did wonder whom the old man might be phoning at this ungodly hour in the morning, but whoever it was, she was in no doubt. The topic of conversation she was about to hear was of great concern to her and the boy.

Kathy wasn't in the same room as the old man, but she was only feet away, so with her ear to the door, all she had to do was listen. And when the telephone receiver was picked up at the other end, she recognized the voice immediately and in due course, heard every word that was spoken.

"What on earth are you playing at?" Said Pennington gruffly. "Have you any idea what time it is"

"I'm sorry." Gerald insisted. "But I had to speak with you. We've got a problem. The boy's arrived… but Kathy's here as well."

"Yes. I know." Pennington was indignant. "Jack phoned me earlier from a call box and told me what happened."

"There was nothing I could do?" Gerald persisted. "I couldn't send her back… could I?"

"No of course not." Pennington agreed somewhat reluctantly. "Just humor the woman. Keep her happy. She won't stay long, I'm sure. Jack reckons she'll go back home again in a few days, and leave the boy down there with you. And even if she stays a short while, it doesn't matter, she's got to go back soon, otherwise she'll lose her job."

"And are you still coming down here as planned?" Gerald asked.

"I'll let you know." Said Pennington. "I want to be there when the boy does his deed, so you need to keep me informed, and let me know what Kathy intends to do?"

"I'll do what I can." Gerald whispered. "But it won't be easy. She's a bit of a handful."

"You'll do what you're told and obey me… as usual." Pennington insisted. "And I'm sure that I don't have to remind you of your obligations. I want that young woman out of the way. Do you understand me?"

"Yes." Said Gerald solemnly. "I understand."

And as Gerald replaced the handset and dimmed the light, Kathy slipped away back along the corridor, and within seconds, was back in her bed curled up with the boy.

When Kathy peered out of the bedroom window the following morning, the first thing she noticed was a small strange looking man hanging around at the end of the lane. He was shabbily dressed and much like a tramp, but from what she could gather, he was there for a reason. It was too far away to decide what he was doing, but nevertheless, she was suspicious.

"You're up early Mum." Robert grunted suddenly. "What are you looking at?"

"I'm not sure." Said Kathy somewhat distracted. "There's a chap out there, and he's acting odd?"

"How do you mean?" Said the boy.

"I don't know, I'm not sure." Kathy sounded perplexed. "Why don't you take a look?"

Robert sighed. "Do I have to?"

"Yes you do." Kathy insisted. "We need to get up anyway and see what old grumpy is up to?"

And as soon as she mentioned the old man, there he was trudging down the lane, towards the stranger, away from the cottage. It was only seven o' clock, but apparently Grandpa Gerald was an early riser and he seemed more than eager to speak with the man. The job of gatekeeper had many facets, and dealing with rogues and ruffians was only one of them.

"I see what you mean." Robert gasped as he dragged himself out of bed and stared through the window. "He's only small, but he looks tough."

"Yeah. That's what I thought." Kathy agreed. "A bit like you then eh?"

Robert smiled.

They carried on watching as the two men talked and then, just as their clandestine meeting came to an end, Grandpa Gerald handed over what looked liked a fistful of banknotes, just as he'd done with Kathy the previous evening, before she went to the shop.

The two men shook hands, the stranger turned away in the direction of the village and Gerald headed back towards the house.

"I wonder?" Said Kathy dubiously, as she slipped away from the window. "What was all that about?"

"I don't know?" Robert whispered. "But I'm going to find out."

With breakfast over, and whilst Kathy was washing the dishes, Robert began his search for Grandpa Gerald. Their host hadn't been seen since his presence earlier in the lane, and the boy was intrigued. He'd had an interesting chat with Gerald the previous day, but there were still lots of things he wanted to ask the old man. The cottage itself was of modest size, but the plot in which it rested was at least four or possibly five acres in total. An undulating piece of real estate with lots of woodland, numerous big trees and several outbuildings dotted here and there among the clearings.

And as Robert wandered around with prying eyes, he saw the man emerge from an old Nissen hut, only a few yards from the cottage, and immediately Gerald locked the door behind him. It was a relic from the Great War, all but concealed behind an abundance of unruly, rebellious weeds.

"Good Morning Robert." Said the old man sleepily. "So. What are you up to?"

"I was looking for you." The boy smiled cheekily. "Are you busy?

"I'm always busy." Gerald insisted. "But if you want to talk again, I'm always here."

The boy was mindful of huge bags below the old man's eyes, seemingly much larger and darker than the day before. Grandpa Gerald looked sad and tired, but more than anything, he looked bewildered.

"The castle!" Said Robert suddenly. "At Aberlleiniog… I want to go there?"

"And I want to show you something." Gerald sighed wearily as he plucked the key from his pocket and unlocked the hut once more. "Come on lad…step inside… you need to see this."

Robert followed him cautiously, wondering what on earth the old man had in mind. He wasn't frightened of anyone including Grandpa Gerald, but he was apprehensive of what might be lurking in the old pre-fabricated shelter with its rusting semi-circular shaped roof and filthy concrete floor.

The old building had a power supply, but when Gerald threw the light switch, the single flickering forty-watt bulb only emphasized what a godforsaken place it was. Littered with what could only be described as metal cages, snares and booby traps, and barely an inch of floor space that wasn't covered in medieval security devices. A stockpile of assorted contraptions with steel springs and armed with jagged teeth, perfect for the capture of any would-be poachers and trespassers alike.

"So. This is it Robert." Gerald whispered grimly. "This is the reality of what you're up against."

"I don't understand?" Said the boy. "What has this got to do with me?"

"Everything." Gerald grimaced. "And these are only a few of the things that people have used on this side of the void."

"To do what?" Robert asked defiantly.

"To stop the travellers." Gerald insisted. "The time travellers. No one wants them here. Not here… or anywhere!"

"But you got through." Robert challenged the old man. "And so did dad?"

"We were lucky." Gerald pleaded. "That's all."

"And so am I." Said the boy. "I'm lucky. And apart from that, I've got you to help me… and you're the gatekeeper."

"That's true." Gerald agreed. "And I can tell you everything you need to know. But what I can't predict is what sort of medieval monstrosity might be waiting for you on the other side. And not only that, its what kind of reception committee you're likely to encounter. Assuming of course, that you manage to negotiate your way through the wormhole in the first place?"

"But why does everyone hate the time travellers?" The boy was unconvinced. "I still don't understand?"

"There are lots of reasons." Gerald growled. "And most of them can be linked to some sort of prejudice and discrimination. But the main cause for concern… is fear… of disease."

"What kind of disease?" Said Robert warily.

"You name it." The old man groaned. " We've had Measles, Cholera, Typhoid, even Leprosy, and at some point in time, almost every disease known to man. Throughout history, numerous pandemics have ravaged humanity, and the danger is that one day a traveller will arrive here with Smallpox or Bubonic Plague or something else so contagious that mankind might be wiped out altogether. Just think about it. It's a real possibility. And my job is to see that doesn't happen. So… if you did manage to go back in time, and somehow, against all the odds, do what my brother asks. And in the process…contract some kind of hideous disease and bring it back to the present day. It would leave me no option… and you Robert, and anyone else involved, would never be allowed to leave this place… ever again."

As they stepped outside, back into the sunshine. Robert's features and mood had changed, as if he already knew what kind of future awaited him. But despite their conversation, he didn't hate the old man for what he'd said, because if anything, it was needed. Gerald's comments were important and honest and left the boy under no illusions. Grandpa Gerald had offered to help the lad if necessary, but if things went wrong, there would be serious repercussions.

They walked towards the cottage, each of them completely absorbed in their own thoughts, and it was then that Kathy suddenly appeared.

"Gerald. I need a word please?" The young woman beckoned. "Have you got a minute?"

Gerald flinched a little, no doubt wondering what was coming next. "Of course." He answered eventually. "What can I do for you?"

"I need to use your telephone, if that's okay?" She asked. "… And speak with my boss at the pie shop."

"Oh… okay." Said Grandpa Gerald somewhat reluctantly. "Is there a problem?"

"No. I don't think so." Said Kathy confidently. "Although I can't imagine he'll be too pleased when I tell him the news."

"Really?" Said Gerald. "What's that then?"

"I've decided that I'm not going back. Not yet anyway." She insisted. "And if he doesn't like it, he can stick his job, it's as simple as that."

CHAPTER 11

What Kathy needed was sleep. She'd hardly slept a wink since her arrival at the cottage, so after another warm day, an encouraging telephone call with old Mister Burton at the pie shop and a hearty supper, she decided on an early night. The boy wasn't ready for bed, not yet anyway, so he gave her a big hug, promised to be quiet when he turned in, and curled up on the sofa to read his book. The old man's rocking chair meanwhile sat idly in the corner. In normal circumstances Grandpa Gerald would have seesawed back and forwards in it for most of the evening. The ragged old carpet underneath was a testament to that, but instead, he was busy in the kitchen, messing with a couple of fishing rods. He felt stranded in his own house with nowhere to go, although you'd never have guessed. He wasn't used to company and it made him uneasy, but it wasn't all bad news, and on the upside, Kathy's cooking was something he could get used to.

And despite his anxiety and loss of privacy, he was determined to keep the boy entertained as best he could, and offer the lad a distraction to what was really on his mind. And a few hours on the beach, the following day, casting feathers for mackerel would no doubt, do exactly that?

By midnight the property was in darkness, with only the faintest sound of a tawny owl, somewhere in the distance, struggling to penetrate the iron curtain that engulfed the cottage. A deathly lingering silence where no one stirred and no one made a sound, until first light when Kathy opened her bleary eyes and reached out to touch the boy. And he wasn't there.

She was drowsy, and the boy's absence didn't register, not immediately anyway, but then all of a sudden she realized instinctively what it meant and sat bolt upright in her bed… the nightmare had begun.

She clambered out of bed, dashed into the hallway and shouted for the boy, screaming at the top of her voice, demanding a response, but all the while, knowing he wouldn't answer.

"What's the matter?" Grandpa Gerald groaned as he dragged himself out of his bedroom. "Where is the boy… where's he gone?"

Kathy's vision narrowed as she glared at the old man.

"There's only one place he would have gone." She yelled. "And we both know where that is, don't we Gerald?"

The old chap nodded reluctantly. "The castle… at Aberlleiniog." He declared. "But please don't worry. I've got someone down there. He'll stop the boy before he gets into any trouble… you'll see."

"Do you reckon… really?" Kathy sneered. "If you believe that Gerald… you're mistaken, he might be young but trust me, he's not stupid. And I've got to tell you… you don't know him… and you have absolutely no idea what he's capable of."

The young woman understood the boy better than anyone, and already he'd been gone an hour. With a small khaki coloured canvas bag over his shoulder that he'd taken surreptitiously from the cottage, and a big stick grasped firmly in his fist, he looked every bit the intrepid adventurer. He'd a mile or so to walk to the castle, but with the absence of light, the trail was difficult to follow, and despite his well-made plans, very quickly lost his way. And as he trudged around in the darkness, he tripped and fell headlong into a stream. Robert wasn't injured, but he got a good soaking in the process along with the shoulder bag and its contents.

Undeterred however, he got back on his feet immediately and very soon rejoined the path, a gentle slope heading away from the village and down towards the coast. At times easy to negotiate, but every so often, overrun with dense vegetation and brambles, that snatched at his shorts and jerkin and severed his flesh. Though eventually as the minutes passed and scattered light filtered through the trees, the route ahead was obvious. And suddenly in the distance, he could see the ghostly shape of Castell Aberlleiniog, peering majestically through the early morning mist. A modest ruin of what was once a Mott and Bailey castle, before the current building was completed in the seventeenth century. Not a fairytale castle by any means, but still a mysterious brooding structure, skulking in the shadows at the first blush of day.

Suddenly the boy froze on the spot.

Robert expected company and was well aware that Grandpa Gerald would have someone on site 24/7 but what he didn't envisage was a brush with one of Gerald's men, so early in his quest. But sure enough, about fifty yards dead ahead, unless mistaken, there was a man squatting down at the side of the path. He'd propped himself up, his back resting against a low stonewall, his feet pulled up underneath him. It was the small tough looking brute that Gerald had spoken to the previous morning. One of three lieutenants the old man employed on regular shifts, to guard the entrance to the void. Their job, to deter anybody gaining access to the wormhole, but more importantly, to prevent the passage of any would be interlopers from the past, securing a toehold in 1955.

And if any locals or visitors got nosy or hung around too long, there was lots of ways that Gerald's men would persuade them to move on. On most occasions, their presence alone was enough to convince people to stay away, but if that didn't work, threats of physical force or actual bodily harm would quickly follow.

Robert still didn't move, but then again, neither did the thug, and as the minutes passed, the youngster wasn't sure what to do, but then all of a sudden, it occurred to him, that maybe… just maybe, the man was dozing at his post?

He eased his way forward deliberately along the path, placing one foot in front of the other, determined not to make a sound. And as he got closer to the ruffian, the man let out the faintest of murmurs, not dissimilar to a flag fluttering in the breeze, and a very gentle snore confirmed what the boy was already thinking. The gatekeeper's sentry was fast asleep, and consequently, any arrival at the castle would be unopposed.

If he lingered, there was a chance the man might wake and seize him, but if he hurried before the sun revealed itself, and the colors of the forest became more intense, then no one could stop him. So… exactly like Kathy, on the first night at the cottage, the boy moved stealthily, negotiating the quickest and safest route away from the menace that he'd stumbled upon, and very hastily, he made himself scarce.

And as the distance between them increased with every step, Robert's rendezvous at the castle drew ever nearer. He could see the structure quite clearly as it reappeared time and time again through the gaps in the trees. And finally as he stepped into the clearing, it was there in all its glory, bathed in a soft mellow light, waiting to be explored.

In the eleventh century when Robert of Rhuddlan ruled the whole of North Wales, the castle's moat was full of seawater, replenished twice a day with every incoming tide. But by 1955 the sea had receded almost a mile, and a huge hollow encircled the old fortress, articulating its magnificence. Robert clambered down into the depression and very quickly scaled the other side, where he then gained access into the castle itself. A mythical coffee coloured structure and a wondrous exhibit from ancient times. And somewhere very near was a secret labyrinth, a wormhole, where travellers could enter and risk everything in search of a better future, either that, or take a voyage of exploration into the past.

So…once inside he scurried around the battlements, looking down at the fields below and eventually… he saw what he was looking for. Only a matter of yards from the rear wall stood a mighty oak tree, at least a hundred feet tall, with a girth of thirty-eight feet and six inches. It was nine hundred years old and according to Pennington, at the center of the main trunk, where the branches head off in their own direction, stretching up and outwards towards the light. At the very heart of the tree, was a rippling vacuous space, only large enough for a child to enter.

The boy gripped his stick even harder. He had a twinge in his gut, unlike anything he'd ever experienced before, but despite the uneasiness, he knew exactly what he was going to do. He'd made up his mind, and that was that. He looked across at the old oak and blinked repeatedly, his vision adjusting to the ever-changing light. The crown of the tree, which he would have to negotiate, was at least twenty feet from the ground. And somehow he'd have to scale that height without a ladder, and as far he could determine, without any obvious toeholds. He couldn't access the old girl from the castle itself, so after a few deep breaths, he set off and sprinted back the way he'd entered the building. In due course circumnavigating the castle, until eventually he reached the base of the tree. It was simpler now to decide on a route, but nevertheless, it wouldn't be easy. He'd climbed lots of trees before, like most young lads his age, but nothing compared to this gnarly old beast.

He searched frantically for something to stand on, at least to get him off the ground, but that proved pointless. Gerald's men had got wise to people trying to climb the old tree, and anything that could be used for that purpose, had been removed from the site. Although the one thing the boy could do was to use his penknife to cut notches into the bark at suitable positions, and that's exactly what he did.

In comparison to the size of the colossus he was trying to conquer, these were barely scratches on the surface of a monster tree. And yet... these same tiny gouges, would hopefully, assist the boy's skinny fingers and a size three shoe, as he tried to scale the mighty oak.

The stick was surplus to requirements now, so inevitably, he left it at the base of the tree. The knife he put back in his pocket, but just in case, he left the blade exposed.

And after a long deep breath, he started his ascent.

Robert scrambled up the first few feet without too many problems, but as he got higher, the exercise became much more difficult, and there was little or nowhere to secure a hold on the tree. He hung on desperately, and gradually bit-by-bit managed to squirm up a little further to a section of the trunk that offered a few more toeholds and at that very moment when he reached out to grasp what appeared to be a firm niche on the old beast. He howled in agony as the full force of his discarded staff clattered down on the back of his legs, and brought him crashing down.

The boy hit the ground with some considerable force and immediately he gasped for breath. He was dazed but not unconscious and as Gerald's watchman dragged him over onto his back, a spurt of bright red blood trickled slowly from between the boy's lips.

"You little runt." The man screamed in his face. "So… what's the plan then… eh?"

"What?" The boy struggled to speak. "What do you mean?"

"You boy!" The thug bellowed loudly. "Who the hell do you think you are?"

Robert mumbled something in response that's for sure, but whatever it was, it was indiscernible.

"I didn't catch that?" The man screamed. "So go on… tell me again, who are you?"

Robert eased himself up slightly and at the same time slipped his hand into his pocket.

The man leaned over him, eager to hear what the boy had to say for himself, his stale breath very evident, his body odor inescapable.

"Who am I?" The boy snorted suddenly. "You really want to know, don't you? Well then… I'll tell you, shall I?" The man glared at the boy somewhat bewildered.

"I'm the butcher's boy." Robert screamed at the man. "And this is just for you."

The boy dragged the penknife out of his pocket and stabbed the man directly through his left boot. Robert pulled the blade out immediately, and in a flash he punctured the man's right foot as well, even more viciously. The thug fell to the ground in an instant, clutching his injuries, blubbering like a baby. The boy got to his feet, picked up the canvas bag, put the knife back in his pocket, and for a second time, began to climb the tree.

Kathy wasn't far behind. She'd abandoned Grandpa Gerald on route, because he couldn't move fast enough. But when she heard the shouting up ahead, she wasn't close enough. She had the castle in her sights, but when she reached the clearing and saw the old structure for the first time in all its fullness, Robert had already scaled the old tree and at that very moment was literally staring down the barrel. Pennington had described it as a "rippling vacuous space" and that's exactly what it was. A fusion of time and space where wars would be won and lost, fortunes made and squandered, lives would change forever, sometimes for the better, but often not. And make no mistake, concealed within this swirly soup, the vultures circled, always on the move, never resting.

The boy scrambled to his feet to get a better view and marveled at what he saw. Yes it was scary but more than anything it was fascinating. And as he stared into the whirlpool, he could hear the faintest of sounds. He leant forward, edging ever closer, and like the bronze-age seafarers off the coast of Sicily, lured to destruction through the sweetness of the sirens song. He slipped inside the void and disappeared completely.

And only a few moments later, Kathy hurtled around the castle wall, battle ready, desperate to find her boy. At the base of the old tree was Gerald's watchman, still sprawled across the grass, clutching his bloodstained feet, having tossed his boots sky ward. He was whimpering and cursing loudly, insisting what he'd do to the lad, if he ever saw him again, and as far as Kathy was concerned, that wouldn't wear.

"Was that your kid?" The man yelled. "Was it? I'll kill him."

"I don't think so." Said Kathy firmly. "And there's a good reason for that."

"Oh yeah." He mouthed. "And why is that then?"

The young woman grinned of a fashion, but there was more than a glint of humor in Kathy's inauspicious stare. She bent down slowly and reached for the big stick.

"You wouldn't dare?" He screamed. "You wouldn't bloody dare."

"Oh I dare." She urged him on. "And what my lad did to you…was nothing."

Kathy grasped the stick tightly at one end with both hands, raised it high above her head, and brought it down hard on the miserable wretch. The man put his hands up to try and protect himself, but after numerous savage strikes, his resistance diminished. She never intended to kill the man, but if the stick hadn't broken, she may well have succeeded. And no amount of blows would compensate her, for what he'd said about the lad.

Kathy left the man in a sorry state, but it was all he deserved, and given half the chance she swore to finish the job, if he ever crossed her path again.

Then very quickly, she turned her attention to the tree. She'd listened in to enough conversations to know exactly where the boy had gone, and anywhere he could go, she would follow. If the boys could do it, then so could the girls, and that included climbing trees. And subsequently within a few minutes, she too was staring straight into the void. Kathy did hesitate and crouched down for a while in a similar way to what the boy had done, mesmerized by what she could see. But after a short while, she'd seen enough and eventually allowed herself to fall forward and slip inside.

CHAPTER 12

Kathy sank rapidly as cold sticky moisture covered her from head to toe, and immediately she gasped, her lungs burning, desperate for air. And the tide, if that's what it was, continued to pull her under, its waves rolling in and out, its rhythm constantly changing, and in the distance, lights flickered on and off, some of them spectacular, others hardly noticeable. Trapped in a maelstrom of air that ebbed and flowed, and like a piece of driftwood in a whirlpool, she was helpless to resist. And each time one of the brighter lights came closer. Kathy flailed her arms frantically above her head. As if marooned on a desert island, desperate to attract the attention of any passing ship, that might appear fleetingly on the horizon. And in the confusion, the awful realization that Robert was in the same predicament… had he suffered the same fate… she might never find out?

But then as quickly as it began, suddenly it was all over. And Kathy's bruised and battered body was cast aside forcefully, away from the void and up onto the wet grass. She put her hands out to break the fall and the pain shot up her right arm like a fire. Coughing and spluttering she got to her feet. Every bone in her body ached like crazy, her vision was clouded and bleary, but despite everything, she was eager to find out exactly where she was?

And the first thing she noticed was a strong smell of wood smoke. That and other less attractive odors, not hard to recognize, but seemingly more acute than anything she'd experienced before, and if she wasn't mistaken, the sound of an incoming tide.

She pivoted a full circle very, very slowly and when she'd done, it was abundantly clear, this was indeed Aberlleiniog, but not as she'd seen it, just a short while ago. The stone structure had all but gone, and in its place a recently constructed Motte and Bailey castle, a wooden fort on a large mound of earth with numerous buildings at its base. An entire settlement surrounded on all sides by a deep expansive moat, full of brown foamy water, fed straight from the sea. Kathy wasn't aware of how far she'd travelled back in time, and in a way it didn't matter, all she was bothered about, was that Robert had arrived in the same place, at the same time. And in that regard, she needn't have worried. This was an important day in the year of our lord 1093, and young Robert Rudd had turned up at the castle only minutes earlier. The only problem was, he'd been arrested already, and unless he could explain himself and where he'd come from, he was in serious trouble. Lying in wait for the boy was a group of individuals loyal only to the indisputable Lord and Master of the whole of North Wales. Namely one Robert of Rhuddlan. And as they dragged the lad off to the bailey, kicking and punching, it was touch and go as to whether he might ever be seen again.

Kathy's arrival had been less memorable, and after all the excitement and hullabaloo that had gone before, she strolled off towards the entrance to the castle, with little more than a flicker of interest from a passing Norman knight. The man's grey woolen tunic almost hidden from view, his bright red cape breezing along behind him, his muscled legs and leather sandals splattered with mud.

Kathy's eyes were trained on some invisible object up ahead, and she was struggling to focus, when suddenly, the man moved back into her line of sight, and touched her cheek gently with the side of his thumb. She looked up immediately and scowled at the man.

He had a small swatch of reddish blonde hair on the top of his head, while the back of his skull was closely shaven. And as he glared at Kathy with eyes as blue as a mountain lake, he looked more Scandinavian than Norman.

"You have a wonderful mouth." The man grinned. "What's your name girl?"

Kathy held the man's stare, but after a few seconds, turned her head towards the ground, and walked away.

"Have no fear lass." The knight laughed. "I will find out. And then… I'll hunt you down."

Kathy moved on quickly, making sure that she wouldn't have to endure his gaze again, and dashed towards the castle.

And as the boy had already discovered, life inside the bailey was noisy, dirty and very smelly. At Aberlleiniog it consisted of a modest piece of ground to the south of the keep, with numerous buildings crammed quite close together. A jumble of structures including stores, kitchens, barracks for the Norman troops and stables. And that's where Robert was, until a decision could be made, as to what to do with him. In normal circumstances any young whippersnapper such as young Robert Rudd would have been severely reprimanded. But as far as the Normans were concerned, the lad was a mystery. He'd appeared out of nowhere, his clothes looked ridiculous and he sounded absurd. And although his captors were a hardened band of brothers, not unwilling to hand out some serious punishment when needed. They thought it might be prudent to seek advice from their Lord and Master, and see if he might wish to question the boy.

So as Kathy picked up speed and headed inside, determined to avoid unwanted attention, she was pleased that it was crowded with lots of people, pushing, shoving and shouting. And no one else seemed particularly interested in her. It was market day, and a lot of farmers from the country had come to Aberlleiniog, loaded with all sorts of produce such as cotton, grain and vegetables. She squeezed her way through the rabble, in the direction of the stables, surrounded by the essence of unwashed bodies and an abomination of a smell that was wafting across from a makeshift fish stall. At that point, completely unaware that Robert was only a matter of feet away.

When suddenly, all hell broke loose. Someone took his eye off the boy, and he was gone. Robert dashed out of the stables as if a swarm of killer bees was after him, and he wasn't going to stop. And it's doubtful that any of his captors would have caught him again, if someone hadn't got in the way, but they did, and that person was Kathy.

In an instant both of them tumbled to the ground in a flurry of arms and legs. Crashed out on a squalid dirt floor, littered with horse-dung, fish guts and entrails. And from that moment on, the game was up…

It was obvious they knew each other, and in a heartbeat a number of Norman soldiers surrounded them. One seized Robert, and dragged him to his feet. Kathy screamed and she too grabbed the boy, and refused to let him go. Then suddenly, one particular individual stood directly above her, and as she looked up, all she could see was a giant hand stretched out and coming towards her. It was the knight who'd spoken to her outside the castle, only this time she couldn't ignore him or his gaze. She was groggy and felt like she was floating, but as the man clasped her wrist and pulled her up, she wondered immediately. Was he rescuing her from the mob, and if so, what would he want in return, if anything?

"So. I'll ask you again." The man urged. "And this time I suggest you answer me. What is your name girl?"

"It's Kathy." She whispered.

The knight took hold of the boy and immediately the others backed away. "And this?" He demanded to know. "Who is this?"

"His name is Robert." Kathy answered immediately before the boy had chance to open his mouth. "He's my son."

The knight smiled suspiciously. " I don't believe you. You don't look old enough."

"Well that's up to you." Kathy insisted. "But its true."

"And how old is the boy?"

"I'm ten." Robert chirped in, unable to contain himself.

"He's nine." Kathy insisted. "He tells lies."

The knight sneered.

"Whether he's nine or whether he's ten, it doesn't really matter does it?" He sniffed. "What's more important is where you've come from. And what you're doing here at Aberlleiniog?"

"We've come to see Robert of Rhuddlan." The boy croaked. "We've got some information for him."

"Oh is that right?" The knight sniggered. "Well that's a shame, because he's really busy at the moment."

Everyone apart from Kathy and the boy burst out laughing.

"He's expecting us." Robert shouted. "And if you don't take us to him straight away, you'll be in trouble."

Kathy stared at the knight with some trepidation. One look at the man's eyes, told of a lifetime of struggle. Was she foolish enough to think that one cheeky kid and his bedraggled mother might convince the man to change his mind? She didn't think so. But in an age of valor and chivalry, the boy's boldness could not be ignored.

"So. Where is all this information?" The knight asked. "Can you show me?"

"I had a bag." Robert insisted. "They took it off me?"

The man glared at the mob. Most noticeable was his refusal to smile or show any warmth towards his comrades. Roger de Montbray was well known for his fiery temper and would explode at the slightest provocation. He released his hold on the boy and stepped towards them, and sure enough within a few seconds, the boy's small khaki coloured canvas bag had appeared from an outstretched arm and dropped to the ground.

"Show me." The knight growled as he turned to face the lad. "And this better be good… or else."

Robert knelt down beside the bag to untie the straps, but almost immediately it was obvious that he was struggling. The straps had swollen, and it took him forever to get the damned thing undone. And when finally he did get it open, he was taken aback. He tipped the bag up on its end, and watched in horror as the contents slid to the ground in a heap of sludge. His birth certificate, the prized color photograph of Skipton

Castle and the H.G. Wells novel all ruined and unrecognizable. Unbeknown to the boy, when he'd fallen into the river on his way to Aberlleiniog, the bag had filled with muddy water. In normal circumstances the contents may have survived, if only for a few days, but after the fall, Robert had entered the wormhole. He'd travelled back in time, for the best part of a thousand years and consequently the boys highly prized documents had disintegrated. All the proof that he needed… had vanished completely.

The knight looked over his shoulder as if he already knew how the crowd would react, and he was right. It was the odd voice at first, but very quickly a torrent of abuse came in from all sides, and before long they were shouting for blood. The situation deteriorated quickly and only one individual stood between Robert and the mob, and that was Roger de Montbray. A ruthless mercenary with a hunger for power, a desire for wealth, and as luck would have it, a fascination for the boy's mother.

When all of a sudden, Robert stepped up and hollered as loud as he possibly could.

"Please. Listen to me. There's something I want you to see, and its very special."

And with that, he stuffed his hand deep inside his pocket.

"I challenge you." He shouted. " All of you…has anyone seen anything like this before."

Immediately the crowd went quiet.

All the boy had to do was pull his hand out and show them whatever it was that he was ranting on about. And he did exactly that, but like a magician in the midst of a trick, he prolonged the mystery, and kept them guessing. There was a danger to what he was doing, and a good chance he might be accused of some kind of sorcery. But at long last he pulled a clenched fist out of his pocket, and suddenly, all the attention and a hundred pairs of eyes focused in on the boy's hand. Robert uncurled his fingers very slowly, and exposed the big reveal, a five-blade penknife with a wooden handle. A precision cutting tool with several sharp blades, and each of them made from a high quality stainless steel, nonexistent in the eleventh century. And it looked exactly as it did in 1955 when he first stole it from Skipton market.

He opened each blade in turn for everyone to examine. "See… I told you didn't I?" The boy shouted confidently. "And it's a gift… for Robert of Rhuddlan."

The knight was fascinated. He stepped forward and immediately snatched the instrument from Robert's hand, eager to examine it and get a better look.

"Tell me?" He growled. "Where did you get this from?"

"At Skipton." Said the boy confidently. "When I went to visit the castle."

"You've been to Skipton castle?" Said the knight in disbelief. "When was this?"

"A few weeks ago." Robert insisted. "It was amazing."

The man looked down at the youngster with some incredulity, unable to make sense of anything the boy said.

"And how did you get there?" He whispered cynically.

"Someone gave us a lift." Kathy interjected before the boy could answer. Increasingly concerned that Roger de Montbray was asking too many questions. And the more questions he asked… the more difficult it was to answer.

"It's a long way to Skipton." He insisted. "I find it hard to believe."

"Well its true." Said Kathy. "So can we speak to Lord Rhuddlan now please… and give him his gift?"

"That might not be possible." The knight snarled. "I haven't made my decision yet."

"Its important." Kathy stressed. "Its vital that we give him some information, and if we don't see him soon, it'll be too late."

The knight glared at Kathy and then at the boy. He was visibly shaken, angered that anyone dared to question him. But at the back of his mind, a nagging suspicion, that what they were saying might be the truth?

In the end however fate played its part, as a thunderous yell reverberated throughout the whole of the castle. It was a man with powerful lungs and the voice of a foghorn, and as young Robert Rudd had recently discovered. "A man used to getting his own way."

And he was standing at the base of the keep, his legs shoulder width apart, his hands on hips and thumbs turned back in a dominant display of authority, elbows flaring out on either side. Appearing much bigger than he actually was, the famous Norman adventurer and the Lord of all North Wales, Robert of Rhuddlan.

And at his side Robert's lapdog, the long-suffering but faithful brother, with a lifetime obligation to support and defend him, was Gerald.

Both men were easy to recognize and both of them looked incredible.

Each wore a close fitting tunic with a mantle or cloak over the top. The cloaks were made from the finest cloth and lined with furs, Gerald's was crimson and Robert's a deep vibrant reddish purple. And just a glimpse of the man was enough to put the fear of god into any individual, Norman or Welsh.

Totally different from the last time that Kathy and the boy had seen him. They'd waved him off at the Waterhead pier on Lake Windermere in 1955 when the man was seventy-five years old. An old chap looking very distinguished, with large silvery whiskers, tweed jacket, burgundy coloured waistcoat and baggy corduroy trousers. But now in 1093… the man was in his prime, late thirties, at the height of his power and one of the most formidable men in the kingdom. And like many of his fellow Normans, he was clean-shaven.

And when he addressed his fellow knight… Roger de Montbray was compelled to respond.

"Who are these people?" Lord Rhuddlan demanded to know. "And what is that in the palm of your hand?"

"It's a gift… for you my lord." The knight insisted. "This youngster and his mother have brought it for you."

"Is that right?" Lord Rhuddlan grinned at Robert as he took possession of the knife. "It looks interesting. Where did you get it lad?"

"At Skipton." Said the boy. "We went to see the castle."

"I like it." Lord Rhuddlan grinned. "But why give it away. You could have sold it?"

"We had to speak with you." Robert assured him. "There are things you must know."

"Then talk." Said Rhuddlan abruptly. "And let's hear what you've got to say."

"Excuse me please." Kathy interrupted. "But is it possible that we can speak with you in private?"

Lord Rhuddlan glared at Kathy. He wasn't used to being challenged, especially by a woman, and as many of his subjects had often learned, it wasn't wise to rub him up the wrong way.

"It might be prudent." Gerald whispered.

Lord Rhuddlan nodded. He was irritated but sensed the importance of what he might learn. "Of course." He growled. "Follow me."

CHAPTER 13

Life inside the keep was every bit as smelly as it was elsewhere in the castle, but at least now they'd escaped from the mob. Even Roger de Montbray had been excluded, much to his annoyance, and only Kathy and the boy would get the opportunity to visit the Great Hall and speak with Lord Rhuddlan and his brother.

After climbing the steps they entered the hall itself through a screened passage at one end. It wasn't that great and it wasn't that large. A rectangular room three times as long as it was wide, and much higher than one would expect. It had windows on one of the long sides that looked out over the bailey. A multifunctional room where Lord Rhuddlan would eat and entertain, and at night often as not, a number of his servants would sleep on the floor. It had a central hearth, with the smoke from the fire rising up into the roof space and out through a vent. And the hearth was used for heating, but also for cooking, and over the fireplace was a large overmantel and plasterwork containing Lord Rhuddlan's coat of arms.

"Sit down." Gerald insisted. "I'll get one of the lackey's to bring us some drinks."

"I need to go." Kathy urged him. Is there a toilet?"

The two men looked bemused.

"Over there." Gerald pointed towards a curtain at the far end of the room, where a crude privy allowed the occupants to relieve themselves. It was a garderobe that jutted out from the side of the keep. A hole in the wall allowing human waste and anything else that Lord Rhuddlan might want to dispose of, to drop into a pit at the bottom. Where subsequently by means of a crudely dug channel, it would find its way into the moat. Kathy scurried across the hall and dragged the curtain behind her whilst the others waited patiently. And as soon as she returned to her chair, the boy decided that he also needed a pee. And all the while, Robert of Rhuddlan tinkered with his new gift, whittling away at a rough piece of timber, amazed at the sharpness of his latest pocketknife.

"We've got wine, water or beer?" Gerald announced. "Just help yourself."

"Is the water safe to drink?" Kathy asked.

"It's not from the river, if that's what you're thinking" Gerald sighed. "Its rainwater. We collect it in a special container on the roof. But its up to you, do as you wish?"

Lord Rhuddlan placed the knife down on the table and stared at the youngster.

"I have to say, you look very familiar boy." He grunted. "Have we met before?"

"Yes." Said Robert fearlessly.

"When was that, remind me?

"In the future." The boy declared. "We spent a full day together in 1955."

Robert of Rhuddlan was not a man to be messed with. They called him the butcher. He had a reputation as tyrant and land grabber and of all the Normans who dared to occupy this part of Wales... he was the most hated. He regarded most people as complete fools, but despite his intolerance to others, on this one occasion, his gut feeling was to listen.

"I don't understand." Lord Rhuddlan argued. "You better explain."

"I know all about you." Robert insisted. "You told me things. Things that I couldn't possibly know... unless we'd met before?"

Gerald laughed.

"Is that right?" Rhuddlan sneered contemptuously. "What sort of things?"

"I know where you were born and how old you are." Robert smiled confidently.

"I doubt it." Said Lord Rhuddlan. "But I am listening carefully. So go ahead... but if you get it wrong lad. God help you."

"Calvados in Normandy, France." The boy growled. "In the year 1055... so by my reckoning. That makes you thirty-eight years old... Am I right?"

Rhuddlan didn't flinch he leaned back in his chair, and took a mouthful of wine from his glass.

Gerald just stared at the boy, his eyes unfocused and a little wild. Kathy could see that the man wanted to believe what her little boy was telling them, but couldn't come to terms with what was being said.

"And you have a book." Said Robert. "A manuscript with lavish decorations. It was part of the Book of Kells and what is often described as the missing pages from the Gospel of Saint John. Is that true?"

"You are well informed boy, I'll give you that." Lord Rhuddlan muttered. "But what of it?"

"You sent me here." The boy stressed.

"And why would I do that?" Rhuddlan took another sip.

"Because you want the book." Robert insisted. "And you want me to take it back to you, in 1955."

"This is nonsense." Said Lord Rhuddlan angrily. "And now… you're wasting my time."

"You told me lots of other things as well." Robert lowered his voice. "About the old Welsh druids and the stories they would tell about certain places where you could disappear, and then reappear sometime later in the future. And one particular place at the base of the castle here at Aberlleiniog, where at low water, there was the strangest of voids. A deep crack in the Earth's surface, one moment its there, and the next, impossible to find."

"Go on…" Gerald winced.

"There's going to be a skirmish at Rhuddlan castle." Robert insisted. "You described it to me as another one of those bloody Welsh uprisings. But somehow you manage to escape and you make your way back here by boat to Aberlleiniog."

"And then what?" Said Lord Rhuddlan excitedly.

"A hundred Welsh warriors will follow you here." Said the boy. "But with only a handful knights to defend the castle. Your only option is to enter the void beneath the castle, and travel forward into the future to escape certain death."

The two men looked at each other in disbelief, and when brothers look at one another like that, nothing good was going to happen.

"And this so-called void." Lord Rhuddlan growled. "Will it take me forward to 1955?"

"No. That won't happen." Robert sighed. "You end up in 1917. And you start a new life… but the main thing is… you survive."

"And my family?" Lord Rhuddlan asked.

"It's complicated." Said the boy. "Gerald will follow you later. And he'll bring along your youngest son John. But you will see them again. I promise."

"So how did you get here?" Lord Rhuddlan snarled.

"Only recently you discovered another void at the rear of the castle, at the base of an oak tree." Said Robert. It has a passage that enabled us to travel back in time, from 1955 to 1093."

"So lets get this right." Lord Rhuddlan grimaced. "In 1955 I must be at least seventy five years old… is that right?"

"Yeah. Thereabouts." Robert agreed.

"So tell me this?" Lord Rhuddlan growled. "Now I know about the second passage, why on earth would I bother going forward to 1917? All I need to do is to enter the void at the back of the castle, and go directly forward to 1955. I'll take the book with me, and if I'm not mistaken, I won't have aged a day."

"You can't do that." Kathy insisted. "That's not the plan."

"I can do what I want woman." Said Rhuddlan. "I'm indebted to you for all the information, but now I'll take matters into my own hands."

"Are you not bothered about your son, or Gerald or the boy?" Kathy screamed. "And the trouble that might cause?"

"Not in the slightest." Said Lord Rhuddlan.

"But I'm your grandson." Said Robert. "I'm the butcher's boy."

"Maybe you are… and maybe you're not." Insisted Robert of Rhuddlan. "But at the end of the day, you're just another bastard child, and one of hundreds. Oh yeah… and I forgot to mention… that skirmish with the Welsh warriors at Rhuddlan castle… you were right… that happened yesterday."

"So what happens to us now?" Kathy cried.

"That's up to you." The butcher grinned. "You can stay here if you wish. But if you want to go forward to 1955… you can join the queue?"

Suddenly someone was banging on the door furiously, and before Lord Rhuddlan could answer, it flew open and a jumble of bodies piled in. Two of them were Lord Rhuddlan's men, and the other was a young woman they were trying to restrain. A big chubby girl with long blonde hair and ruddy red cheeks, very intimidating, and just like Medusa with a nest of venomous snakes protruding from her head. The fat girl had what appeared to be, living braided pigtails that whirled around her as she moved.

It was the girl from Skipton castle. The one who Robert had crashed into and exchanged words with, only a few weeks ago.

"We found her outside." One of her captors shouted. "In the same place that we found the boy. She's trouble."

"Get your filthy hands off me." She screamed. "Or I'll punch you in the face."

The girl was livid and her so-called jailers unable to prevent her from doing almost anything she wished.

Lord Rhuddlan got to his feet in an instant, picked up a poker from the hearth, and started to beat one of the gaolers about the head. The man raised his arms instinctively, trying desperately to protect himself, but eventually he fell to ground, and only then did the punishment cease.

"Get him out of here." Lord Rhuddlan screamed at the other warder. "And if either of you dare to step foot in here again, I will kill you."

The man bent down immediately and grabbed hold of his colleague, and within seconds, they were gone. Leaving the big chubby girl in the center of the Great Hall, now quaking in her shoes, at the thought of what might happen next.

"Are you going to behave?" Lord Rhuddlan asked menacingly. "Or shall I show you what else I can do with this poker?"

"I'll behave… I will." The girl sniveled. "I promise."

"What are you doing here?"

"I don't know." The girl sobbed. "I honestly don't know?

"So… where have you come from?" Gerald growled.

"I was playing hide and seek?" The girl insisted. "And I hid behind one of the gravestones."

"Where was this?" Said Rhuddlan. Still holding the poker tightly in his fist.

"The Holy Trinity Church." The girl gasped. "At the side of Skipton castle."

"And then what?" Lord Rhuddlan asked.

"There was a hole in the ground." The girl was shaking. "I must have slipped and fallen in. But the next minute I was back outside again. And that's when those two thugs grabbed hold of me… This is a castle isn't it?" Asked the girl.

"It is." Said Gerald. "But its not Skipton castle."

"Where am I then?" The girl cried.

"Aberlleiniog." Said Lord Rhuddlan. "You're in Wales."

"Wales!" Screamed the girl. "I'm not in Wales… I'm in Yorkshire."

The girl's pigtails whirled around even faster, her eyes darting from one thing to another.

"Not any more." Said Gerald. "You're a time traveller. Albeit an unwilling one, but nevertheless, that's what you are."

"I don't understand." The girl shrieked.

"What year is this?" Said Lord Rhuddlan calmly. "Do you know?"

"Of course I do." Said the girl. "Why wouldn't I?"

"Go on then…" Said Rhuddlan. "Tell me?"

Its 1955." Said the girl. "And I'll be thirteen next month."

"I'm sure you will… if you live that long." Said Rhuddlan menacingly. "But I've got some bad news for you. You've travelled back in time to the third of July 1093. And now that you're here, you'll stay for as long as I wish it. Do you understand?"

Kathy glared at the youngster and nodded her head, encouraging the girl to do exactly the same, terrified of what might happen if she didn't.

The girl just stared in front and very, very slowly she bowed her head.

"Good." Said Lord Rhuddlan. "Well… that's settled then."

Only moments later, someone else came knocking.

"Pardon me Lord Rhuddlan." Said the man urgently. "But I must advise you. There are two sailing ships approaching Aberlleiniog from the North."

"Do we know who they are?" Said Rhuddlan shakily.

"As far as we can tell." The man gasped. "Both boats are loaded to the gunnels… with Welsh warriors."

"How long do we have?" Said Gerald.

"An hour… at the most." The man insisted.

"And then what?"

"We'll be overwhelmed." The man declared. "We've only a handful of men to defend the castle and the Welsh have gathered a huge army."

"One Norman knight is more than a match for ten Welsh peasants." Lord Rhuddlan answered angrily.

"Maybe so." Said the man cautiously. "But these are trained soldiers armed with long bows and javelin, determined to reclaim their lands and unwavering in their main objective."

"Their main objective?" Rhuddlan laughed dismissively. "Tell me…what might that be then?"

"I daren't my Lord." The man insisted. "To repeat such words would be sacrilege."

"To hell with all that." Lord Rhuddlan spat. "What do they want?"

"They want your head sir." Said the man vehemently. "On the end of a spear."

Lord Rhuddlan dismissed the man and immediately he and Gerald were in deep discussion. It was difficult to hear what they were saying and the mob outside were getting restless. But a few minutes later Rhuddlan had left, and now Gerald was in charge.

"So. Until I say otherwise." Gerald insisted. "The three of you must stay here, and I suggest for your own sakes, you hold your tongue."

"Lord Rhuddlan will need us." Said Robert.

"Did you not hear me?" Gerald gasped.

"Oh yeah. I heard." Said the boy. "But I want to help."

"Really?" Gerald growled. "And why would that be?"

"It's obvious." The boy shouted. "He's my Granddad."

"You hardly know him." Gerald insisted.

"No maybe not." Said the boy. "But I came here because he asked me to, and if I can, I'm going to help him."

Gerald's mind began to wander, acting out different scenarios. Had the boy simply thrown himself into the void and succumbed to the old man's bullying? If so, he understood why. Robert of Rhuddlan was a tyrant and as Gerald had stated many times, he was a man used to getting his own way. Or... was the lad as crafty and manipulative as his Granddad, and had he another agenda? Which ever it was, Gerald needed to be careful, not only for his brother's sake, but also for his own survival.

"Lord Rhuddlan will be back in a few minutes." Said Gerald. "We'll speak to him again when he returns."

The boy nodded.

CHAPTER 14

At the first sighting of warships off the Anglesey coast, every occupant of Aberlleiniog was in fear. Even Roger de Montbray. And as the knight looked out towards the Menai Strait, he felt a trickle of sweat down his back, and tugged at his tunic.

He muttered to himself, still offended that Lord Rhuddlan had denied him entry into the keep, and suspicious of all the recent comings and goings. First of all, the arrival of the boy and his mother, and then the weird looking girl that someone had discovered in the field outside. And what might happen next, was anyone's guess.

He would try to repel the Welshmen when they arrived, alongside any other knight able to bear arms, but if there were any other way, he wouldn't hesitate to take it. The Normans were clearly outnumbered. The Welsh flags on the enemy boats, too numerous to count, hovering in the breeze, as they edged ever closer. The famous red dragon was alive and well, every javelin sharpened, every Welshman persuaded by the task in hand… to put Robert of Rhuddlan's head on the end of a spear.

When Lord Rhuddlan returned to the Great Hall he'd removed his purple cloak and jewels. He looked like any Norman of lower rank, except for the fancy ornate book, tucked underneath his arm, a manuscript with lavish decorations, and according to Robert's dad, a source of unparalleled information.

"The boy wants to help you brother." Said Gerald. "I think you should let him."

Lord Rhuddlan stopped what he was doing and glared at the boy.

"So. What can you tell me, that I don't already know?"

"I can tell you what to expect when you arrive in 1955." Robert insisted. "And where to go."

"Its of no importance." Rhuddlan growled. "I've already got a plan."

"But people will be waiting for you." Said the boy. "You'll be in great danger."

"I don't think so." Lord Rhuddlan unsheathed his dagger and brandished it for everyone to see. "Its others that need to beware."

"You may be outnumbered?" The boy sighed.

"Maybe." Said Rhuddlan. "And if so… the knife will come in handy."

"I was only trying to help." Said Robert. "But it seems like you've thought of everything."

"No… you're right of course. You must follow me… into the void." Said Lord Rhuddlan with a sudden change of heart. "Give me time to get on my way, then follow me… there will be things you can help me with."

"Are you sure?" Said Gerald.

"Absolutely." Lord Rhuddlan agreed. "He's a good lad. We can look out for each other, can't we boy?"

Robert smiled.

"And the book." Said the boy suddenly. "Can I see it?"

Lord Rhuddlan's demeanor was increasingly odd, but at the mention of the book, every muscle in his face seemed to tremble and his stare hardened.

"Its very special. He said eventually. "I will show you… but we must be quick."

He released his hold on the book, placed it down very carefully on the table, and stepped back. It wasn't huge, about fourteen inches tall and ten inches in width, but as everyone in the room would soon discover, size can be deceptive.

"This isn't just a book." Lord Rhuddlan declared. "Its much more than that. In fact, it's lots of things. It's a masterpiece of paper engineering, a work of art, and the brainchild of St John the Apostle. And yet, when it first came into my possession, I never took much notice of it. I had no idea how important it actually was. But then one day, I opened it up, and suddenly I realized… I had the world at my feet."

He leant forward and peeled back the front cover, and an audible gasp reverberated around the Great Hall.

It was a book with three dimensional pages and additional paper elements that could be handled by the reader. It defied logic. Every leaf unfurled automatically across the table, allowing the book to spring, pop and expand its page… and there for all to see was a labyrinth of passages and the story of time travel through the ages.

A triumph of Western calligraphy with sensational lettering in ink from a wide range of substances, some of which had been imported from distant lands, and wonderful illustrations of the world in its infancy and in the future.

"It's a map." Lord Rhuddlan growled. "A map of the earth, showing every land mass and every body of water. And some of the towns and cities, and some of the countries… they haven't been discovered yet? And how is that possible… I don't know?"

"Its beautiful." Said Kathy. "I've never seen anything like it."

"It's a miracle. That's what it is." Lord Rhuddlan gasped. "And I'm going to take this with me forward to 1955."

"Does it show every void and every wormhole?" Asked Robert.

"I think so." Lord Rhuddlan sighed. "But not only that. It shows the opening to each tunnel and where the tunnel terminates, and the period of time that will elapse between entry and exit. Some of the tunnels are short and some are long. Some are large and others tiny. Many are located in clusters, such as here at Aberlleiniog, and yet in other parts of the world, there are none."

"And does it name each location?" Kathy gasped.

"It does." Lord Rhuddlan agreed. "And yet… I've never heard of some of the places. New York, Berlin, Sydney and Wuhan. For some reason they have numerous tunnels. And every one of them has a link to the ancient past and to the future.

Having secured the book for myself and learned of its secrets, it didn't surprise me when you turned up, but now that you have. It's time for me to leave."

Lord Rhuddlan closed the book immediately and got to his feet.

"The enemy is only a short distance away." He declared. "We mustn't delay."

And so… along with a handful of loyal men, they exited the Great Hall, and made their way quickly through the castle, towards the oak tree. It was hectic and noisy and few people paid them much attention. Too preoccupied with their own safety, many of them loading up their carts and heading to the hills. Warriors preparing for the onslaught yet to come, and all the while, the Welsh war drums echoed across the water.

And when they got to the trees, the entrance to the wormhole wasn't obvious. The wind was getting up and everything seemed different. They searched frantically in the undergrowth, but despite all the shuffling of feet and scrambling about in the bushes, there was nothing.

"And this is where you landed?" Lord Rhuddlan growled. "Are you sure?"

"I think so." Said the boy.

"You think so?" Lord Rhuddlan screamed. "That's not good enough. We need to find it… now!"

Its here somewhere." Said Kathy. "It has to be."

"I can see it." Said the boy suddenly. "Below that branch that's slapping at the ground." Robert stepped forward and pulled back the branch, and sure enough, it was the entrance to the void. Once seen, never forgotten, and like a mini-tornado with a vacuum at its center, eager to draw anything and everything into its grasp.

"Right then… You and You." Lord Rhuddlan pointed angrily at two of his men. "Grab hold of the girl." He demanded. "And throw her in."

And much to everyone's surprise, including the girl herself, the big lass with long blonde hair and ruddy red cheeks, never moved. By the time she realized what was happening, Rhuddlan's men had lifted the girl clean off her feet and she was on her way. And as she plummeted headlong into the abyss, her pigtails spun around furiously, but only for a moment, until she disappeared completely along with her screams.

No one spoke. No one dared. But then somewhat predictably Lord Rhuddlan laughed.

"Right… now it's my turn. " Said Rhuddlan. "And if I hurry up, the fat girl might soften my landing."

He clutched the book to his chest as if his life depended on it. And maybe it did? But when he tried to climb inside the wormhole. He was far too big. He tried time and time again but every attempt was futile.

The boy remembered his conversation with Pennington. "The void itself is very unstable" The old man had insisted. And "Its only big enough for a scrawny youth like you."

"Its too narrow." Said Robert suddenly. "You'll never get through."

"Nonsense." Lord Rhuddlan spat. "The girl was fat… and she got through?"

"Maybe so brother." Said Gerald. "But I do believe you might be even fatter."

"So what do I do?" Lord Rhuddlan pleaded. "I need to get away… now!"

"You can head for the hills." Said the boy. "And try again when things have calmed down. Or if you wish… you can hand me the book and I'll take it through for you. I reckon you might be able to squeeze through if you've nothing to carry… what do you think?"

Lord Rhuddlan's eyes narrowed in response. "If you really want to know what I'm thinking boy, then I'll tell you. You're a snake." He retorted angrily. "And that's never going to happen. The book stays with me."

"Well then." Said Robert. "There is only one thing you can do. The tide will be out soon, so if you want to escape, you'll have to use the other wormhole at the base of the castle. Apparently it's much wider than the one near to the tree. So I suggest you get yourself down there, as quick as you can, before a hundred Welsh warriors make it to shore, and if you can manage to do that immediately… you might stand a chance?"

"I don't trust you boy." Lord Rhuddlan screamed. "In fact… I don't even know why you're here?"

"Because you sent me." Robert yelled. "And all I'm trying to do, is what you asked me to do. But the trouble is… you never listen."

"No I won't." Lord Rhuddlan insisted. "And I never   will."
"Well then… so be it." Said the boy. "There's nothing else I can do."

"That's right." Rhuddlan agreed. "So. Get out of my sight… and if you ever cross my path again boy, I'll have you branded."

"Hang on a minute Granddad…" Said Robert daringly. "I've got one last thing that I want to say to you?"

Lord Rhuddlan glared at the boy.

"What happened to my Grandma?"

Rhuddlan rocked back on his heels, appearing like he might fall over at any moment. He was rattled that's for sure, but his face gave nothing away.

"Your Grandma…" He stuttered. "What about her?"

"Where is she?" Said Robert. "Is she here?"

"No…. No she's not." Lord Rhuddlan insisted. "Not any more."

"So. Where is she then?" The boy growled.

"She died." Lord Rhuddlan whispered. "Three months ago… here at Aberlleiniog. It was sudden."

"What happened?" Said the boy fiercely.

"She was poisoned." Rhuddlan alleged. "There was nothing we could do for her."

"Who did it?" Robert screamed. "Tell me?"

"We don't know." Lord Rhuddlan insisted. "It was hemlock…in a drink, intended for me." "And you never caught anyone?" The boy was disgusted.

"No." Said Lord Rhuddlan angrily. "I retaliated… if that's what you are asking. I hung five Welshman outside the castle gates… but no one said a word."

What was she called… my Grandma?" The boy whispered.

"Eleanor." Said Lord Rhuddlan. "And for what's it worth. She was a good woman and I miss her.

Suddenly the sky grew darker as hundreds of arrows rained down on Aberlleiniog. The Welsh boats were only minutes away, and the castle now in range of the archers. Anyone caught in the open was in trouble, and there were many. In their wisdom, a handful of Norman knights mounted their horses and raced towards the beach. They had every intention of repulsing the enemy as they stepped off the boat, but it wasn't to be. The Welsh arrows were notoriously powerful at short range and ravaged both horses and men. One Welsh arrow struck the leading rider with such force that it penetrated his armor, travelled through his leg and into the horse itself. And as man and beast lay dying on the ground, a second volley completed the slaughter. Lord Rhuddlan scurried off immediately, back towards the castle, still clutching the book. His brother Gerald ran off in the opposite direction. Robert stepped forward once more and pulled back the overhanging branch.

"There's nothing else we can do here." Kathy assured him. "We've got to leave." She kissed the boy gently on the cheek then threw herself headlong into the abyss. Robert allowed her enough time to disappear completely… then he too plunged in after her.

For the first time in his life, Robert of Rhuddlan was alone. He ran for his life like all the others, but with each new deluge of incoming arrows, he leapt for cover. Cringing like a coward under an upturned stall… numb with fear. And there were others close by, in a far more precarious position, groaning from their injuries. One old man in particular, howling like an animal caught in a trap, his foot completely shattered by a stray projectile. A flock of ravens screeched loudly from the castle walls, no doubt gathering together to decide the man's fate. Lord Rhuddlan turned his head away. He didn't care. All that concerned him was the void at the base of the castle, and his need to escape.

But eventually when he got there, the seawater was sloshing against the rocks, and he had little option, but to lower him self down into the sea, and hopefully find the opening. He held the book at arms length, high above his head, fearful of the consequences should he slip below the waves. And it was then that Roger de Montbray emerged suddenly from between the rocks and waded towards him. He punched Lord Rhuddlan under the jaw with his fist, then stepped back immediately, no doubt waiting for the book to fall from Rhuddlan's grasp… but it didn't.

He charged forward yet again and punched Rhuddlan three more times, once to the side of the head, and twice in the face. Lord Rhuddlan stumbled, blood rushing from his nose, but still he refused to go down.

"Just hand me the book." The knight screamed. "Or I'll beat you to death."

"You traitor." Lord Rhuddlan mumbled. "You'll hang for this."

"I don't think so'" The knight scoffed. "That's never going to happen."

And he was absolutely right.

The javelin hit Roger de Montbray directly in the chest with tremendous force. It entered the knight's rib cage and ripped through his body, the tip of the weapon emerging through his backbone, the razor-sharp barb oozing with blood. He staggered backwards a few feet then dropped suddenly into a sitting position, only his head remaining visible above the water. It was ridiculous that he didn't fall over to one side… but he didn't. The man's piercing blue eyes wide open, his heart undoubtedly as black as ever, his body in limbo. Propped up inside the rock pool, rocking from side to side in a channel of bluish-red liquid, replenished continually by the lapping waves and Roger de Montbray's stuttering heart beat.

Lord Ruddlan teetered back on his heels, his head spinning, desperate to keep the book dry, and somehow he managed to hold it up away from the water, as yet another spear flew past his head. Then as luck would have it, he saw the fissure for the very first time, and immediately edged his way towards it. A deep crack in the Earth's surface where the old Welsh druids would disappear and then often as not, reappear some time later in the future. He clambered up and out of the water and wandered aimlessly into the abyss. He was seconds away from being captured, and in the confusion, it was Roger de Montbray who assumed Rhuddlan's identity. So eager were the Welsh to claim their prize, they cut off his head and stuck it on the end of a spear.

Inside the void it was desperately dark, but up ahead there was a light. Rhuddlan pushed on and tried to get near it. But just when he thought he'd found his way through, the light dwindled. A second light then appeared even further away, so once again he advanced, but every time he got close, the same thing happened. And suddenly three lights, and he didn't know what to do. He lunged forward straight ahead and amazingly he was out in the open. Only he wasn't at Aberlleiniog castle any more. Instead he was up to his neck in sludge. And he wasn't the only one.

He could hear men screaming for help, but no one came. He'd taken a serious beating from Roger de Montbray, and never realized that what he was suffering from was concussion. He was also well and truly stuck, and only for the corpse underneath him, he'd have disappeared completely and never re-emerged.

He lay there motionless until it went dark, then crawled out on to a wooden duckboard, leaving every fragment of eleventh century clothing in the mud. And at that point after stumbling over a man's body, a soldier that had just been killed fighting with the second battalion of the Border Regiment. He undressed the chap, put on his uniform, rolled him over into the mud and watched carefully as the body disappeared into the bog. It was April 1917 and Robert of Rhuddlan had turned up at the battle of Arras, close to Vimy Ridge. And all he had to do now was to crawl back towards the British lines, having assumed the dead soldiers identity… that of Allen Pennington.

CHAPTER 15

Kathy's escape from Aberlleiniog was fortuitous, but dangers still remained.

As she'd dived headlong into the void, she closed her eyes and begged God to spare her and the boy. She'd been frightened of entering the wormhole in the first place, but even more scared of losing Robert, and one thing Kathy would never do... was to imagine life without him.

Unable to stop her self from falling, she descended quickly into a maelstrom of hot air, and when finally she opened her eyes, all she could see was a billowing purple mist and what appeared to be a feint yellow light flickering in the distance. But sadly, despite her prayers... there was no sign of the boy. She longed for him to be there, to put her arms around him and smother him with affection. But it was never an option. Then suddenly she realized the full horror of the situation. Kathy had no idea where Robert might be and not a clue as to where she might be headed, a long way from home, shrouded in mist and lonelier than she'd ever been. The smog was inescapable. And as the vortex propelled her forward towards the light, the vapor flattened Kathy's hair and trickled down her face. It was hard to make sense of what she was seeing. But eventually as the exit to the portal got larger, she spied a vast expanse of green with sporadic flashes of silver and blue. It was the meadow at Aberlleiniog, swooping down towards the sea, and even further in the distance the silvery shimmers of the Menai Strait. Astonishing colors of gold, purple and pewter. A refuge… and a place to rest and a place to wait… for Robert.

Then at long last after what seemed an eternity, the wormhole was forced to give her up. Not discharged on open ground as she had been on the outward journey, but instead, left clinging to the branch of a nine hundred year old oak, in the shadows of the castle. Completely exhausted and precariously balanced, about fifteen feet from the ground, and a welcoming party directly below her.

"Good. You made it." Shouted Grandpa Gerald assuredly. "So. Where's the boy?"

Kathy didn't have the strength to answer. She swallowed hard but the spittle wouldn't go down and it made her cough, then almost immediately she gasped. And then she fell.

For a brief moment she was airborne, as one of Gerald's accomplices hurried forward to catch her. But despite the man's best efforts, he couldn't reach her, and she hit the ground face first with a loud sickening thump.

Meanwhile Robert's chance to escape the battle at Aberlleiniog would be dashed. It suddenly occurred to him that Lord Rhuddlan was always destined to make it through to 1917, and if not, then events would have taken a different course, and the boy wouldn't even be there. And… when they'd parted company, only a few minutes earlier, Rhuddlan was clutching the

Book of Kells closely to his chest, determined at all cost, not to let it go. So… the question was… what happened to the book before Rhuddlan arrived at Vimy Ridge?

And… if he had lost it along the way, why on earth could he not remember?

Consequently, at the very last second, and as the whirlpool lured him in, Robert decided in a flash that he wouldn't follow Kathy after all, so he stuck an arm out, and made a grab for the tree.

Kathy was heading home, forward to 1955, but the boy seemed fated to stay exactly where he was in the year of our lord 1093. And at that very same moment, when Robert decided to abort his journey back to the present, a hundred marauding Welshmen stepped ashore at Aberlleiniog.

If he'd left it a moment longer, the boy could not have hung on, and inevitably he'd have followed his mother into the wormhole. But once he'd made his mind up, he refused to succumb to its power, and a few moments later, crawled away into the undergrowth, even more defiant than before.

He knew that Kathy would be mortified when he didn't arrive close on her heels, but in a way, things might be easier. He loved his mum dearly, but now, he only had himself to look out for, and in Robert's mind, that made everything a lot simpler.

When Kathy opened her eyes, she wasn't sure where she was, and struggled to make out the features of the room. The only sound came from a creaky door, swaying lazily in the breeze. But it didn't take her long, to grasp, that once again, she was tucked up in Grandpa Gerald's snug little cottage. Back in the bed she'd shared with the boy, yet sadly, young Robert was still absent. Kathy had the great grandmother of all headaches and couldn't focus properly. Her head was spinning, her mouth as dry as a bone, but nevertheless, was vaguely aware of at least two pairs of eyes watching her ever so closely. She could hear Gerald whispering in the background, but failed to recognize who else might be sat alongside him, although eventually she realised who it was. An abrupt shift in posture and a sudden swish of the blonde braids that encircled the girls head, had given her away. It was the mysterious lass from Skipton castle. Who somehow, had followed Kathy and Robert back in time, before Lord Rhuddlan and his henchmen, had sent her packing, unceremoniously back to 1955. She'd started her journey in the grounds of the Holy Trinity Church, at the side of Skipton castle. And after a brief but terrifying journey back in time to 1093, now found her self returned to the present, but a hundred and fifty miles from where she'd started, at Aberlleiniog castle in North Wales. And if the girl's agitated state was anything to go by, clearly, she was desperate for answers.

Kathy's eyelids flickered momentarily as she tried to clear her head and immediately, the girl began to question her.

"I want to go home." The girl sobbed. "You've got to help me… please?"

Kathy tried to position herself higher up in the bed and as she leant forward, Grandpa Gerald placed an extra large pillow between her shoulders and the headboard. It was a noble gesture on Kathy's part, but evidently, it was all a bit too much. And the truth was, she wasn't well. Badly bruised from head to toe, she had the face of a china doll. Any natural colour in her lips was non-existent, and as the nausea overwhelmed her, once again, the world went black.

Robert meanwhile was trying hard to evade the Welsh troops, as they disembarked at the foot of the castle. He rolled into a natural hollow in the ground, and proceeded to pull leaves and sticks over himself, until at last, it would have been hard to spot him. But the Welshmen were everywhere. He lay there as stiff as a corpse, his heart in his mouth, for what seemed like an hour, or maybe more. Until eventually the urge to drink something, anything, dominated his thoughts,

And then to make matters worse, he suddenly realised that his legs were covered in ants, and when he tried to brush them off. The angry little buggers took great offence with any attempt to move them on. He wanted to jump up and sweep them all away, but knew that any involuntary movement, a gasp or a scream would draw attention to himself, and it was anyone's guess, as to what the Welsh troops might do with him, if he was discovered?

But it wasn't just the men he had to hide from, it was the dogs too, and when one nosy mutt came close, its ears erect and its tail held high in the air, the boy froze. It began to snarl and then suddenly a low guttural intimidating sound emanated from between its jaws, and the game was up.

"Well let me see now." One of the Welsh raiders suddenly growled as he dragged the branches away from the boy's hidey-hole. "What on earth have we got here then?"

Robert got to his feet as quick as a flash and ran.

The Welshman was startled and took a step back, before lunging in with both hands to try and get a hold on the boy. But those tiny few seconds made a huge difference and despite all the swearing and shouting, the boy just carried on. The soldier could never have caught up with Robert, but the dog might. Yet strangely after a few feet or so, the hound gave up, and returned to its keeper and understandably a tirade of abuse.

Make no mistake, Robert knew exactly where he was heading, and somehow, by hook or by crook, he would get his hands on that book. He'd already made his mind up to follow Robert of Rhuddlan into the void at the base of the castle, and if that meant shadowing him all the way to 1917, that's exactly what he would do.

And it didn't take him long. The area was full of men weary from battle, and now that the castle had been over-run and all the Norman troops had either perished or taken to the hills, no one seemed too interested in a bedraggled young boy as he scampered by. And most of the Welsh warriors seemed too pre-occupied with their newly acquired prize, and as far as they were concerned, the successful conclusion to their raid. Robert of Rhuddlan's head on the end of a spear, proudly displayed at the entrance to the castle. Although unbeknown to them, it was actually the decapitated head of Roger de Montbray.

Robert jumped into the shallow water and waded between the rocks, searching for something he knew was there, but worried that it might not be that simple to find. And as he explored each nook and cranny, it wasn't long before he gained the attention of yet another nosy soldier, who demanded to know what he was doing. The boy ignored the man, and even when the Welshman decided to climb down into the water, the lad just carried on as if he couldn't hear any of the obscenities that were aimed in his direction.

Fortunately the boy's tenacity was well rewarded, when suddenly he saw the phantom-like fissure trembling in front of him, inviting him in. And before the soldier could grab him, and drag him out onto the rocks… Robert had disappeared.

The water erased his footprints immediately, as he stepped slowly into the abyss. It was dark, very dark, then suddenly he saw a flash of light up ahead and instinctively rushed forward believing that he'd found the way out. But exactly as old man Pennington had described, when he got closer, the light dwindled, and receded further back into the hillside. Then all at once, the light split into three and Robert didn't know what to do. He stumbled slightly and when that happened, he kicked something on the ground and shifted it forward to his right. The boy dropped to the ground and felt ahead with his fingers, completely unaware of what it might be. Then unexpectedly, he placed his hand directly on top of the object… and intuitively he knew what it was.

It was the Book of Kells that Lord Rhuddlan had dropped on his way through the wormhole, and what was often described as the missing pages from the Gospel of Saint John. After the beating that Lord Rhuddlan had endured at the hands of Roger de Montbray. Rhuddlan had suffered a severe concussion, and consequently he hadn't a clue where he'd dropped the book. Evidently, it would have remained there forever, until some intrepid sole had come along and found it. Lord Rhuddlan had lost it, but somehow fate had played its part, and subsequently his own grandson had discovered it.

Robert got to his feet once again and held the book close to his chest, almost in the same way that Lord Rhuddlan had done, when he too had stumbled into the void. So the question was…what next?

He couldn't go back, that wasn't an option. And likewise it wouldn't make any sense to follow Lord Rhuddlan over to France in 1917, nor take the route that Grandpa Gerald had followed to Aberlleiniog in 1918. Which left the boy only one alternative. He would take the path that neither of the other two had chosen, and wherever that delivered him, then so be it?

CHAPTER 16

As he emerged from the wormhole, nothing could have prepared Robert for what was to come, and immediately his life was in peril. Germany was ravaged with war, full of broken people and broken dreams. And on the 28th, April 1945, Berlin was unquestionably the most dangerous place on Earth.

The boy crawled out from beneath the rubble into a scene from hell. He looked across at the ruined landscape, his face frozen with fear. He was still a child, but nevertheless had no illusions. This was all about staying alive, and nothing else mattered. It was a role he'd been given, and later, somehow, if he managed to survive, his thoughts would catch him up. He ran for cover into the rear of a huge building, completely unaware of where he was heading. Germany was on its knees and one of the few places the boy would find refuge, was inside the famous Reichstag, the historic parliament building of the German state.

The soviets had launched their attack on the city a few days earlier, both from the South and the East, and by the end of the month, would surround the city completely. With an army of more than a million men, the outcome was inevitable. The beleaguered Nazi garrison was on the brink of defeat. It would prove to be the last major offensive of the war in Europe, and undoubtedly one of the bloodiest battles of all time.

And caught up in the middle of it all was little Robert Rudd, living on his wits, hiding in the shadows, and most importantly, still clutching Lord Rhuddlan's book, fiercely to his chest.

After weeks of prolonged bombing by both the Soviets and the Allies, much of the city was simply rubble, and most of the houses uninhabitable. So it was hardly surprising that when he got inside the old parliament building, he wasn't alone. Lots of civilians had decided that this was a safer place to hide, rather than remain in their own homes, and consequently, hundreds of stinking bodies were huddled together inside the crumbling structure. Robert scurried off along the passage away from the entrance, until eventually he found his own place to rest, at a reasonable distance from all the others.

He'd cheated death, at least for the moment, but couldn't escape the sound of tremendous explosions and terrible echoes that followed each and every bomb blast. Instinctively like everyone else, he sat down with his back to the wall. It was the obvious thing to do and probably the safest.

Unfamiliar with this new environment, he didn't realize that many of these poor souls had been languishing in the old building for weeks, refugees in their own country.

And after a short while, a little girl aged maybe five or six, wandered down the corridor towards him, pointing her torch in Robert's direction. The batteries were obviously running low, and the soft yellow beam kept flickering and fading as she waved it from side to side. The child looked quite disheveled, but still, she was very pretty, with unruly swirls of long blonde hair drooping down across her face. Then suddenly, the torch failed completely, and the whole room seemed unnaturally dark, as if it had been drained of all light. And straight away, the girl ran off, back to her mother.

It wasn't long though, before she was back, and this time had an old metal cup in her hand, full of ersatz coffee. Robert sat up immediately. He was parched. And when she held the cup out in front of her, for him to grab hold of, he grasped it eagerly with both hands, and gulped it down. He hadn't a clue what it was, and didn't really care, it was hot and wet, and that's all that mattered.

Robert waved at the girl's mother to thank her, and eventually she smiled then turned away.

Without Rhuddlan's book, the boy may well have perished in Berlin, and no one would have been any the wiser. But as Robert knew all along, the answer to his unfortunate predicament was literally at his fingertips, and all he needed was the space and the light to examine it. So when the girl left him alone for the second time, he slinked off along the corridor and clambered up several sets of stairs in search of somewhere more appropriate.

And a few floors higher he found exactly what he was looking for.

A huge oversized table, littered with dust and debris. But even more convenient, an old military style kerosene lamp in the corner of the room, full of fuel, and alongside it, a dry box of matches. In the circumstances, it was nothing short of a miracle. He cleared the wooden surface immediately, and lit the old lamp. And very gradually he turned up the brightness then placed the book down in the center of the table. It wasn't a huge book, about fourteen inches tall and ten inches in width, but as Robert was well aware, size can be deceptive. The old parliament building was shaking continually from the ceaseless bombing outside, but the room itself seemed warmer now, bathing in a ghostly golden light. Robert leant forward ever so slowly and tentatively he peeled back the front cover. His eyes wide open, but his brain unable to respond fast enough to take in all the information. And what followed was a rare moment, when the boy's face was blank with confusion, at a loss for words, until eventually, a small smile played across his lips.

The moment Robert opened up the book, every leaf unfurled automatically across the table, allowing every insert between the pages to spring open and expand. And exactly as Lord Rhuddlan had bragged, back at Aberlleiniog, it wasn't just a book. It was a masterpiece of paper engineering and a work of art. It defied logic. A labyrinth of paper passages and the story of time travel throughout the ages. A triumph of Western calligraphy, with sensational lettering in numerous colored inks, many of which had been imported from distant lands. It was a map of the Earth, showing every land mass and every ocean, in its infancy and in the future. And most importantly, listing every void and wormhole. The entrance and exit to each and every tunnel, where they could be found, and the direction of travel, either back into the past, or forward into the future. And often at the entrance to each tunnel, a footnote, offering a snippet of information about the tunnel's destination.

Some of the tunnels were relatively short, but others stretched from one side of the globe to the other. And many could be found in clusters around certain locations, such as Aberlleiniog in North Wales and if the boy was right… Berlin.

He studied the map in great detail, and from what he could see there were four separate tunnels in Berlin, all in close proximity and near to the center of the city, and each one of them, with access to a different location elsewhere on the planet. One wormhole crossed the Atlantic to Washington, offering access to the U.S. capital in April 1863 at a time when the American civil war was in its third, but bloodiest year.

A second void offered a direct route to Rome, Italy in the year 40AD when the Emperor Caligula was in power. A frightening prospect, but realistically, not an option the boy was ever likely to take.

A third was the tunnel that he'd accessed already from Aberlleiniog in 1093.

And a fourth, if the map was accurate, was a time tunnel located on the roof of the Reichstag, connecting the German capital to Buenos Aires in Argentina. The exact destination was the basement of the Casa Rosada building, the main office of the Argentinian president. It offered a direct route, the same timeline, and hopefully a safe reception on arrival.

And looking ahead with a huge amount of optimism, the boy could see another wormhole between Buenos Aires and Wuhan in China. It was a route that went forward into the future to 2019, with access to Wuhan city, only a week before Christmas. And in the same location, yet another tunnel from China back to Aberlleiniog in North Wales. Offering Robert one final journey that would take him back in time to Aberlleiniog in North Wales. Arriving at the castle in the summer of 1955, only hours after he'd begun his quest, to recover Lord Rhuddlan's book. And the very same day he'd travelled back in time to the year 1093, leaving one of Grandpa Gerald's men, sprawled out in the meadow, blubbering like a baby.

So now there was a plan and as far as young Robert Rudd was concerned, it was perfect.

And if he managed to pull it off, Robert would achieve what old man Pennington had begged him to do from the beginning. Securing Lord Rhuddlan's coveted book in the eleventh century, and single-handedly bringing it forward to the present day.

But first, he would have to get access to the roof.

Robert closed the book very, very carefully, allowing each leaf and every expanded page to fall back into its rightful place. Then with book in one hand and a kerosene lamp in the other, he headed skyward. It was a dangerous journey. He'd studied the map in great detail, and as far as he could make out, the wormhole was situated in a cupola, a dome-like structure at the top of the building. And the nearer he got to the roof, the louder the sound of battle. On some floors of the old building there were bits of heraldic statues and monuments scattered across the floor. It was the end for an old Germanic culture, in the process of being destroyed piece by piece, by an ever-increasing number of in-coming missiles. Finally as he neared the top of the very last staircase, a cacophony of sound resonated across the rooftops. He could see the sky up above. It was black, and any rays from the sun eclipsed by the enemy bombers flying overhead. And the landmark cupola had all but disappeared.

Robert was bewildered. He didn't know what to do. But once again, fate would play its part. And as he stood there seemingly very much alone, looking out across the war torn city, a group of men charged up from behind and literally knocked him off his feet. They never saw him, or didn't care, but either way, it was fortunate they came along. Robert didn't know exactly where the entrance to the tunnel was, but these men certainly did, and one of them looked strangely familiar.

The first two were storm troopers, huge individuals, hand picked, specially trained and armed to the teeth. The next chap was smaller, quite rounded and gasping for air. The last, very dapper and much more assertive, had black pinstriped trousers, a dark blue overcoat, and his hair combed back very neatly. He appeared relaxed like he was off to the theatre. And as he passed the boy, an incendiary device exploded in the distance, illuminating one side of the man's face and mustache. Robert could not have been closer. It was a group of high-ranking Nazis, on their way to Argentina.

And staggeringly… one of them, looked exactly like Adolf Hitler.

The men marched over to the center of the roof, to where the cupola once stood, and one by one they disappeared into the void.

And a few seconds later, the boy followed in their footsteps, and not a moment too soon. A 500-pound cluster bomb exploded in exactly the same spot where Robert had been standing. And an area the size of a football pitch was saturated with thousands of tiny but deadly pieces of shrapnel. Had the boy remained where he was, he would have perished. But immediately he'd stepped inside the time tunnel, the walls closed in around him. He was on his way to Buenos Aires, and nothing could stop him.

It was a different kind of wormhole, much larger than anything he'd seen before, as dark as coal, and only one tiny white light flickering faintly in the distance. Windy too, and the strength of wind increasing all the time, until eventually, a huge wall of air began to push him along. It was crazy and chaotic, exactly like a fairground ride, and as he hurtled through the tunnel, rich scents wafted through the air.

And finally when the tunnel discharged young Robert at the Casa Rosada building in Buenos Aires, there was a welcoming party in the basement, despite the fact that nobody knew he was coming. Robert slinked off to one side immediately. What these people wanted was a glimpse of the Fuhrer, and from what the boy could see, they were not disappointed. There was a large German community in Argentina, and many high-ranking dignitaries had turned up to welcome him. There was lots of heel clicking and countless Nazi salutes, and whilst all that was happening, Robert sneaked out of the building and into the street.

It was a glorious day in Buenos Aires with bright blue skies and warm pleasant temperatures, a far cry from the war-torn streets of Berlin. A dynamic city, full of amazing architecture, steeped in tradition, and as Robert looked back at the Casada Rosada building, its walls shimmered brightly, a wonderful shade of pink. He felt awkward and conspicuous. The streets were busy with people, but he had nowhere to conceal the book. His small khaki coloured canvas bag may have done the job, but that was long gone. And even that may not have been suitable. So as a consequence, he carried the book everywhere, clutching it to his chest, as if his life depended on it… and it did.

He had a mile or so to get across town to an old church called the Mazana de las Luces, where hopefully, if everything went to plan, he would find the next time tunnel. So when he heard the sound of an old streetcar clattering along on its rickety rails and a bell clanging in the distance. He suddenly realized that if he could find a street map and a timetable, it might be a lot safer if he jumped on board one of the trams. And sure enough, up on the high street, there was a tram stop and a schedule, and a list of places of interest situated within the city. The only problem was, it was all in Spanish. And to make matters worst, the boy was penniless.

At the end of the twentieth century, most of the streetcars were horse drawn, but since 1897 many of them had been converted to electric. And now in 1945 the Buenos Aires tramway was the most extensive in the world, with over five hundred miles of track. All Robert had to do, was get his hands on a few pesos, and find the right tram to take him to the Mazana de las Luces.

He wandered along the street, away from the tram shelter, scouring the gutter for a few discarded coins, but seemingly, he was out of luck. That is… until he heard the blind man on the corner, and the unmistakable sound of a piano accordion. The unfortunate chap had placed a black beret on the floor, directly in front of him. And inside the hat there was a few coppers, but evidently, business had not been good.

Robert sat down on the sidewalk only a few feet away, and immediately, it appeared that he was with the blind man. And strangely enough, he wasn't that uncomfortable. After centuries of constant footfall, the huge expansive pavement was warm, smooth and polished. The boy was tired though, and hungry, and a warm wind of hot spicy aromas hung in the air. Most of the smells came from the street vendors and food-stalls only a short distance away, but once again, without funds, he couldn't board the tram and he couldn't eat.

Suddenly a stranger stepped forward and tugged at the blind mans sleeve. The old chap stopped playing, and the moment he did, a large white sandwich was thrust into his hand. The musician thanked the pedestrian calmly and praised him for his kindness. The stranger smiled then placed yet another sandwich, into young Robert's clammy palm. The man had a distinctive smell of alcohol about him, but as far as the boy was concerned, he didn't give a dam. Robert couldn't speak a word of Spanish, and didn't even try, but what he did do, was offer the man a huge angelic smile.

The man grinned, put his hand in his pocket, and placed a few small coins on the ground alongside Lord Rhuddlan's precious book.

The boy had never experienced such selfless behavior, nor had he seen such a large sandwich ever in his life. And as he tucked into his multi-layered, crust-less white bread sandwich with cheese and ham, he pondered the future and what came next.

CHAPTER 17

He was only nine years old, but ever since he could remember, Robert had fantasized about travelling the world and living somewhere exotic, that or playing in goal for Manchester United. He hated the council estate in Lancashire. And just like his mother, he loathed a British system that neglected the working class and provided for the well to do. Buenos Aires was different, unlike anywhere he'd been before, exciting and full of energy. It had rich architecture and a strong cultural heritage. A combination of wide leafy avenues and extensive parks, but most of all it was warm, and despite having never been to Argentina, he had a strange sense of recollection. He'd never seen anything so spectacular. An intoxicating place where a fit young lad like Robert Rudd would either grow up very quickly or perish in the process, but more importantly a place he might call home.

That was… until the man with a strong smell of liquor on his breath came back, and made a sudden grab for Rhuddlan's book. Robert had noticed the chap rushing back towards them, and thought it odd, but never imagined for a second, the man intended to rob him.

If too much drink had encouraged the man to chance his luck, it did nothing to improve his hand eye coordination. He slipped, stumbled to one side and in the process, charged headlong into the blind man. The old musician clattered to his knees still clutching his instrument, and sadly, the lush romantic sound of the piano accordion came to an abrupt end.

The boy didn't wait to see what happened next. As a group of onlookers gathered, he seized the book with both hands, and ran. Robert hadn't a clue where he was headed, but eventually he was back at the Casada Rosada, at the Eastern end of the Plaza de Mayo. Where he found himself pushing against a tide of tourists, milling around the cafes that lined the square. It was then he saw yet another tram stop, packed with people, and a huge route map of the city.

And immediately he noticed the Mazana de las luces on the street map, about two kilometers and five stops away. And in the distance, an approaching streetcar loaded with passengers, with as many bodies on the outside of the vehicle, as there were on the inside. The trams were a symbol of the country's rich diversity of culture, language and religion, and the cities most popular mode of transport. It was impossible to imagine Buenos Aires without trams, and as the vehicle came closer, it was clear, the old tramcar was insanely overcrowded.

And for young Robert Rudd the challenge was to board the streetcar before it stopped. Time his jump to perfection and leap inside the coach before grabbing hold of a door handle, or failing that, the arm of another passenger. Not an easy task with Lord Rhuddlan's book tucked underneath his arm. But at the last minute… Robert held back and watched many of the would-be travellers push their way onto the tram by throwing themselves forward and inevitably onto the person in front. And as many of the existing passengers were overwhelmed with even more commuters, people on both sides of the scramble were pushed, slapped and verbally abused. The boy waited until the tram moved off again, and as it did so, the wind dropped ever so slightly. And it was then that Robert snatched his opportunity, throwing himself forward onto the footplate. He skidded along on his heels, completely out of control then somehow, miraculously he reached for the grab-rail, and everyone cheered.

Somewhat reminiscent of the day on Lake Windermere, when Missus Pennington's favorite hat was swept away in a mini whirlwind. Robert had chased it frantically, for the full length of the boat and at the very last moment, plucked it out of the air. The old ladies brushed-wool hat with feather trim was returned to its very grateful owner, and all the passengers had shouted for joy.

And as the old streetcar trundled away from the Plaza de Mayo, the boy was safely on board, or so it seemed, and so was the book. The ticket collector had given up completely. Robert was surrounded with people, all herded together aboard the vehicle, and as it weaved and meandered its way through the suburbs. A cacophony of screams, screeches and yelps pierced his eardrums. Kids, adults and tourists alike, all shouting at the top of their lungs, shaking and trembling, they were so excited. Dozens of flushed, exhausted faces stared at the boy, some of them quite menacing, which only strengthened Robert's resolve. To hang on to Lord Rhuddlan's book, come what may. So as they neared the Monserrat neighborhood and the Manzana de las Luces, it was crucial that he held it even closer.

Robert's exit from the vehicle was every bit as dramatic as when he first jumped on board. He launched himself from the tram at the first opportunity, denying any would-be muggers who might be plotting against him. The book was something special, anyone could see that, and what the boy couldn't do, especially now, was to let it out of his sight. And the moment his feet hit the ground, he sprinted off immediately, towards his next somewhat notorious location. The Mazana de las Luces had a checkered history, originally a church and home to the early Jesuit missionaries. And since those early days, had been added to over time, providing all sorts of other functions. It had been a school, a library and even a museum. Yet despite its many uses, was still re-known for one particular thing… its mysterious subterranean tunnels that linked each of the cities churches underground.

At the start of the nineteenth century, during the Argentinian War of Independence, the tunnels had been used to store ammunition and provided an escape network for the rebels. But the scariest tales about the Mazana de las Luces concerned the large vaulted underground cells that served as inquisition-style torture chambers in the fifteenth century. It was a large building and the stuff of legends. And how a little boy like Robert Rudd was supposed to find his time tunnel in such a vast network such as this was hard to comprehend.

But despite the angry shouts from an over zealous official, he raced on through one of the huge stone archways that surrounded the building, determined to make it inside. And true to form... he did exactly that.

The caretaker, or whoever he was, soon gave up chase and all Robert had to do, was keep moving. He had to find somewhere to reopen the book, and hopefully, pinpoint exactly where he needed to be. When suddenly, he spied a young man up ahead, striding along quite quickly, and strangely... it made sense to follow him. A heady aromatic fragrance lingered in his wake. He was Chinese. Tall and slim, good looking, with short black hair, his skin a warm yellow ochre, smooth and unblemished. And underneath his arm a fancy ornate book, not dissimilar to the one that Robert had been clenching to his chest for who knows how long?

And one thing was for certain. The boy had no idea where he was going, but the Chinese guy certainly did.

The absurdity of what Robert was doing seemed ridiculous. Yes... the man was Chinese, but that meant nothing. The boy was clutching at straws and knew it. His only real option was to consult Lord Rhuddlan's book once again, and the sooner the better.

Yet before he had chance to do anything, the man disappeared along a narrow, poorly lit corridor. Robert waited for a short while then followed slowly. He wasn't frightened of being seen, but preferred to remain invisible. And as Robert stumbled along the old passageway, the more dismal it became. Until eventually, he grasped the metal handrail at the top of a huge spiral staircase, inched himself forward and peered over the edge.

Bizarrely it was much brighter down below in the basement. Where primitive electric wall lights flickered bravely, against the old grey walls. The boy began his descent. And soon discovered how easy it was to follow the chap at a safe distance… with palpable traces of the young man's cologne, still hovering in the air.

He could hear the man's footsteps far beneath him on the metal stairs. And every now and then, the squeal of a sweaty hand, as it snaked its way along the shiny metal balustrade. Then suddenly, those sounds let up as the man reached the foot of the stairs, and immediately scurried off along an old subterranean passage. It was the signal for Robert to get a move on. And the boy didn't hang around. He threw himself down the staircase in hot pursuit, and once at the bottom… stopped dead in his tracks.

A split second later, and he'd have missed it.

The young Chinese man walked forward into a large vaulted underground cell, and as he did so, the void opened up in front of him. He composed himself carefully, stepped forward once more, and moments later… disappeared.

But then all of a sudden, the sound of new footsteps echoed sharply around the otherwise deserted basement. More than one very large individual was coming down the metal staircase, and whoever it was, was in a hurry. The boy had a quick decision to make. The urge to run and hide was overwhelming, but the desire to move on and finish what he'd started, was even stronger. Robert tightened his grip on Lord Rhuddlan's book, and marched over, to where the young Chinese guy had stood. And immediately, he too was on his way. It was the first occasion the boy had travelled forward in time beyond 1955, and what he would discover in Wuhan, in the winter of 2019, was something a lot scarier than anything he could have imagined.

CHAPTER 18

Robert's fourth and penultimate journey, was a different experience altogether. It was as if he'd climbed inside a child's toy. A huge kaleidoscope where the path in front remained level, but the tunnel itself, rotated around him. A wormhole that was long and narrow, with black impenetrable walls, and up ahead, an amazing spectacle of animation. A unique focal point, with a complex pattern of coloured glass and tiny mirrors, that swiveled and twisted at the end of the portal. And like everyone else that dared to venture this trail before him, Robert rushed forward, seduced by an abundance of shifting color.

Then suddenly… he burst through the egress at the end of the void, and crashed on to the old stone floor of the Gude Buddhist Temple in Wuhan city. Wedged inside a circular passageway between the inner and outer walls of the Yuantong Treasure Hall. All alone but thankfully unharmed and still in possession of Lord Rhuddlan's precious manuscript. And as he sat there basking in the smiles of the Buddha statues all around him, a veil of chalky dust covered his shoes and an earthy scent filled his nostrils. The floor was uneven, worn down by the feet of so many people. Robert placed the book down, opened the cover, and marveled as it rocked from side to side, like a moving picture, every leaf unfurling automatically. It was the third time he'd seen the book in all its glory, but once again, he was taken-aback by its beauty and its splendor. It took a while to determine exactly where he was, but eventually, it all became clear.

He was in the Jianghan district of Wuhan, the largest city in Hubei at the junction of the Yangtze and the Han River. The most populated region in central China and a busy industrial center with a huge network of roads and railroads. In 1927 and again in 1937, the wartime capital of the country and a city of twelve million people. And in order to find the next time tunnel, to enable him to travel back to 1955, the boy would have to make his way across town to the Hankou railway station. According to Lord Rhuddlan's book, about two miles away, in the newer part of the city, close to the Huanan Wholesale Seafood market.

And he was ready to move on. Robert wiped his sweaty palms on his pants and closed the book ever so carefully. Without the book, he wouldn't even be there. But now that he had it firmly in his grasp, it offered him a world of possibilities. He was no different from any other kid. He felt fear like everyone else, but every time it raised its ugly head, he took a step forward, and usually, as if by magic, he found new confidence. For little Robert Rudd the distinction between taking a step forward, or staying put, was everything. It defined him. He stumbled across the exit, and grasped the door latch in front of him. The door opened wide, but as the boy stepped through into yet another narrow walkway, an old lady obstructed his path. She was sprawled out on the floor, seemingly fast asleep, a brick for a pillow. Then suddenly, she turned her head towards him. The boy grinned, and bit his lip. How could he start a conversation, when he couldn't speak the language?

What Robert didn't know, was that naps were common in China, and often as not, people slept in the most unconventional places, even on the street. It was a normal way of living, in a cycle of frenzy and fatigue. They would work very hard with tremendous concentration, then stop suddenly, and go to sleep. And this old woman looked very tired. Robert would never learn how old she actually was, but despite her age, she was fascinating. Her skin was weathered and a lot darker than that of the young man Robert had followed in Buenos Aires, her cheekbones much wider. With short, somewhat rebellious looking hair that could only be described as gunmetal grey, a cute little nose and bright hazel colored eyes. And although her cloths were shabby and her fingers noticeably deformed and twisted, she had the most curious face.

Robert wasn't quite sure how to react. Evidently the old woman was reluctant to move and let him pass, which left the boy only one option. He would have to climb over her.

He took a step back, tightened his grip on Lord Rhuddlan's book then launched himself forward into the air.

The boy was young and agile. Everything he did, was at full power. He couldn't kick a ball without attempting to send it into the stratosphere. And ninety nine times out of a hundred, he'd have got around her without any difficulty whatsoever. But immediately Robert's feet left the ground, the woman raised her knees, and from that moment on, a collision was inevitable. The boy came crashing down on top of her, and it wasn't pretty. China was a busy place where people often bumped into each other, but not like this. By the time the boy had disentangled himself from an awkward situation, the woman's left eye was already swollen, her lower lip trickling with blood. She scrambled to her feet and immediately she started coughing. Whether due to the shock of what had just happened, a viral infection perhaps, or some other reason, she was struggling to breathe. Trying to jump over the old lady was one of the most foolish things the boy had ever done. Robert realized straight away, but it was all a bit too late. He felt sure the woman hadn't broken anything, so in a pathetic attempt to make things right, he started to brush her down with both hands. She didn't respond, not immediately anyway, but the minute he tried to smooth her hair, the woman found her voice, and what followed was a torrent of verbal abuse. He couldn't understand a word of what was being said, but it was the biggest verbal bashing he'd ever endured. He half expected the woman to punch him as well, and anticipating such a move, he held his breath. But eventually his lungs began to pull, for all their worth, to draw in air. And at that very same moment, the woman sneezed with such loudness and suddenness, she whiplashed the boy with a vile discharge that splattered his face. The boy recoiled in horror, grabbed Rhuddlan's precious book and ran off towards the entrance.

It was only from outside the building, that it was possible to get a true picture of what the Gude Temple was all about, an important location of huge cultural value and a mixture of many architectural styles. Although a center for the Buddhists, it had features of the Christian church, the Islamic mosque and God's Temple in Athens. But as Robert soon learned, it was a lonely haven and sanctuary, in the middle of a huge high-rise modern city. Everything else around it was completely overwhelming, and immediately he was claustrophobic. He'd wandered into a huge crowd, full of energy, in a sea of heads, bobbing and dipping, and lots of them chattering away with tiny hand-held gadgets, and what he eventually realized, were telephones. And the sound of traffic, horns honking and engines revving... and so much of it. It was hard to believe. And then suddenly, as if things couldn't get any noisier, the sound of a jackhammer and the constant bleating of sirens. There was a motorcycle snarling at the traffic lights and a full-throated growl from an old truck, belching along in the gutter. If this was the future, it didn't bode well?

The boy knew where he was heading, or so he hoped. The train line that meandered its way through the city, towards Hankou, was very near. At least that's what it looked like, according to Rhuddlan's book. So all he had to do was find it, and follow it all the way to the station, and the only way he could do that was on foot. When suddenly the heavens opened, and the crowds scattered. And almost immediately, it was a rain-washed pavement, where each new step was rewarded with a splash. All good fun in normal circumstances, but the book was at risk, and somehow, it had to be protected. Robert sought shelter at the entrance to a food store, along with several others, and by chance he picked up a plastic carrier bag, put the book inside, and hunkered down to wait for the rain to ease. But twenty minutes later, he was still there, and in that short period of time, the landscape had changed. The sidewalk shimmered, washed clean by a thousand raindrops, the weeds more conspicuous, flourishing in the cracks between the paving stones. A swagger of green in what was otherwise a miserable grey landscape. The road itself, alive with splashes, all kinds of transport chancing their luck on the flooded street. Beads of rainwater skating along their windscreens, the drivers themselves witness to varying sounds of percussion, as huge raindrops bludgeoned their rooftops.

Eventually the rain abated, and when the boy looked out towards the highway, he could see the overhead power lines for the railroad. Strewn across the city like a spider's web, humming with energy. Each one of them connected to the feeder stations, positioned close to the track, and fed with copious amounts of electricity from the national grid. And if he could follow them, back to Hankou, it would take him directly, to where he needed to be… the train station itself, and if he got lucky, the final portal.

So when he ventured outside again, the downpour had stopped completely. And yet the scent of wetness was everywhere. The sun's rays were trying to get through, but not for long, and inevitably, the rain kept on coming. Robert was soaked already. The boy's dark curly locks, that Kathy simply adored, were plastered to his face. But looking on the bright side, the pavement had been abandoned, and in the end, Robert was in no hurry for the rainclouds to vanish. Then suddenly, he saw the answer to his problem, propped up against the wall at the back of the butchers. Bicycles were prolific in China, but this one had everything. It was a small bike, ideal for a nine year old, and it wasn't secured. But more importantly, it had a basket on the front, above the wheel, perfect for Lord Rhuddlan's book.

The boy walked straight over to the bicycle. He jiggled his head from side to side, restoring his normal somewhat disheveled look. Nudged the left pedal to the ten o' clock position, slammed his foot down as hard as he possibly could, and swung his right leg over the seat. Within seconds the bike was racing along the street, like it had a motor. The boy's legs pumping up and down like pistons. And as the front wheel hurtled along on the wet roadway, at an ever increasing speed, it catapulted the rainwater back into his face, more fiercely than it would have, had he continued to walk.

Wuhan was a heavily populated area, full of concrete and man-made structures. Many of which were huge, tall modern buildings, and in the center, the sky towers, intersected by the rivers that flowed through the city. It had a history of serious flooding, but since the building of the Three Gorges Dam, that was all in the past, and what its citizens longed for now, was a better future, free from tragedies and notoriety.

The boy paused for a moment, just to get his bearings, and to look at the view. What he couldn't quite grasp was the size of the silver-grey skyscrapers on the horizon, and why anyone might want to live there? He'd imagined China to be full of rice paddies with most folk working in the fields. But this was 2019 and a lot of these unusual people were condo-dwellers, never raised to take care of so much as a miniature cacti. A lot of their food would arrive in plastic packages, and like any human being, denied their natural environment, they'd head to the parks at every opportunity. Desperate for any open spaces and somewhere they could sit down with their packed lunches and flasks of tea. The wind and rain had blown away the cobwebs and left the streets looking clean, but the boy had seen enough. He didn't want to be there.

And up ahead, close to the train station, there was a worrying development.

A grey haired man about sixty years old, and wearing a facemask, lay dead on the pavement. He had a carrier bag in each hand, and a rucksack on his back. Robert couldn't determine how the man had died, but the reaction of the police and medics, suggested something wasn't right. All the emergency personnel were dressed in full protective suits, facemasks and respirators. It was an image that captured the chilling reality, of what could happen in an overcrowded city, at any moment of the day. And to make matters worse, most of the doctors seemed unwilling to go anywhere near the man. Eventually a medic in blue overalls shrouded the man's body in a blue blanket as they prepared to take him away. Then suddenly a white van with blacked out windows pulled up alongside. The man's body was zipped into a yellow surgical bag, and carried into the van by stretcher. Because of the rain, there were only a handful of passersby, but like the boy, no one dared to go near.

And as the van drove away, the policemen sprayed Anti-bacterial on the ground where the man had lain. The forensic expert, who'd examined the man, removed his protective suit, and immediately was also sprayed with disinfectant by his colleagues. Robert hadn't got a clue what he'd just witnessed, but whatever it was, it looked serious. He realized immediately, he just had to get away, back to 1955. And the sooner he did that, the safer he would be.

And the first chance he got, he pedaled on past the dumpsters at the side of the road, a regular stop over for many of the districts feral cats. It was enough to make his eyes water, the stench from the garbage, lingering in his nostrils. Back in 1093, Aberlleiniog castle had been exceedingly smelly, but this was something even more intense. Robert may have taken a step forward into the future, but after everything he'd observed in Wuhan, he wished it could have been two steps in the opposite direction. And to make matters worse, it started to rain again.

The boy jumped off the bicycle at Station Square, at the entrance to the main building. And it was busy. Crowded with people and jammed with taxis. Much easier to walk with the bike and negotiate all the obstacles on foot, rather than try and weave between them, risking yet another unfortunate collision. And he was still slightly unnerved by what happened at the Gude Temple, unable to believe how clumsy he'd been.

The Railway Station was impressive, a white, very clean looking structure with twin towers at its main entrance, and each tower with its own clock. There was a covered boulevard that extended the full width of the building, supported with large white columns, and behind them, the access to the station itself. After the completion of the high-speed Hefei-Wuhan railway in 2009, Hankou Station had become the main Wuhan terminal for the high-speed trains arriving from Shanghai. And since then, the passenger numbers had increased dramatically, and so had surveillance. He'd have to gain entry into the building, despite the officials and what looked like a security check at the main entrance, and somehow find his way onto the main concourse. The boy had neither ticket nor passport, so the only way he could get inside, was to create a diversion.

Robert got as close to the barrier as he possibly could, without appearing too obvious, still holding on to the bicycle. And at the first opportunity, as a large party of teenagers stepped forward, he grabbed the book, then pushed the bike forward into their path, only releasing his hold on the bike, at the very last moment. The lads were too busy yelling at one another to even notice the pilotless pushbike, and as one individual crashed into the approaching obstacle, at least a dozen others fell over him. It was like a scene from one of Charlie Chaplin's early motion pictures. Which introduced a slower form of comedy than that of the Keystone Cops, characterized by slapstick and embarrassing events. And as more and more people continued to charge forward, the number of casualties mounted and the chaos increased. Security was obliged to get involved, in order to try and sort out the mess, and as they did so, the boy slid underneath the barrier completely unnoticed. Immediately he reasserted himself, placed Lord Rhuddlan's book safely under his arm, and walked off casually towards the concourse.

There were three separate floors at Hankou Railway Station, and what Robert needed now was Level B1. It was the link to the cities subway and if the boy could find it... the link he needed, to get back to 1955.

He quickened his pace. With so much technology about, and a wealth of monitors and cameras on every wall, Robert couldn't be sure there wasn't someone already on his tail. He had a good idea where to look for the tunnel, but until he'd actually found it, he was still in danger. And eventually when he got to the subway, it was packed with commuters.

Hardly unexpected, but as Robert was well aware, the crowds might be a problem. He'd studied Lord Rhuddlan's book at the Gude Temple, very carefully, and what he'd learned, was that this particular void was not hidden away, like many of the others, in some dingy basement. It was out in the open, in the middle of a busy crowded public place, where hundreds of people might congregate, every single day. A ridiculous situation, but one the boy would have to deal with, and proof of yet another distortion of space-time, linking a modern Chinese city with an old medieval castle in a 1950's post war Britain. So the question was... what did the boy need to do, to access the time tunnel, and would the Chinese authorities stand in his way?

He was on the right platform, at the right station, but as he'd always suspected, this last journey would be the most problematic. As the Wuhan metro had expanded into one of the busiest transport systems in main land China, the entrance to the wormhole had been disturbed. It was still there, but it lacked the stability of other more established voids. And if all the tunnels identified in Lord Rhuddlan's book, were compared to the ski runs at any number of winter sport destinations. This particular tunnel would be the most dangerous. Not dissimilar to the famous black-run at the fashionable French ski resort of Val d'Isere, an incredible route down the mountain, known as La Face" with its frighteningly steep descent and monstrous hazards along the way. This tunnel had all those things and more. A sudden collapse of the tunnel would be catastrophic. A collision with yet another time traveller would be just as bad. The boy was in for a bumpy ride.

But all at once, he had a stroke of luck.

Robert had accessed the subway, from one of several escalators, that shepherded people down from the over-ground railroad. There were six of them, lined up side by side. Three of them climbed to the upper floor. The other three clanked along in the opposite direction. And between them, was a wide expanse of space. It separated the handrails, as they moved along at the top of the balustrade, in synchronization with the steps. A huge slope, a meter wide, rising up from the ground at an angle of thirty degrees, and covered in a slippery fireproof cladding. And it was there, half way up the moving staircase, directly above the slope, where Robert noticed something quite bizarre. He watched from the lower platform as one young kid descended the staircase with his mother. He had a tube of soap and water in one hand, and a bubble wand in the other. The kid didn't blow the wand. He just waved it from side to side, and watched as the bubbles soared skyward, captured by an upward current. And whilst most of the bubbles carried on rising, all the way to the upper floor, some didn't, and as far as Robert could see... they didn't burst either... they just vanished.

It was a light bulb moment, but immediately, there were loud shouts behind him, and as he turned his head to see what was happening. The railway officials were almost on top of him. The boy sprinted off as fast as he possibly could, towards the escalator, but instead of mounting the stairs, he launched himself on to the raised section between the handrails. And scampered up towards the void, still clutching Lord Rhuddlan's book, careful not to let it slip between his fingers. His pursuers tried desperately to clamber up after him, but failed miserably. And after several more attempts, it wasn't long, before they themselves became a target of ridicule. Many of the passengers cheered loudly, hoping the lad would get away. They hadn't a clue what he'd done, and probably didn't care. It was just a bit of excitement, in an otherwise boring day. Then suddenly...the boy disappeared before their very eyes, and the place went silent.

CHAPTER 19

Robert was aware of a long dark passage stretching out in front of him. As far as he could tell, it wasn't the easiest or the smoothest of paths, but until his eyes were accustomed to the darkness, he couldn't decide. There was nothing to suggest the tunnel was any different from many of the others he'd used, but instinct told him otherwise, and he could sense the danger.

And evidently there were branches to the wormhole, heading off to the left and right, and some of them, more accessible than the main tunnel. It would have been easy for the boy to follow one, and deviate from where he should be heading, but that was never the plan. He was conscious of the need to stay on the right path, and finish what he'd started. He stepped forward and realized immediately, that once he'd made his move, there was no going back. There was something directly behind him, leaning against him, and whatever it was, it refused to give way. He'd experienced something similar a year earlier, when Jack Rudd bought tickets for himself and the boy to watch Preston North End play Leicester City at Maine Road in Manchester. It was the semi final of the F.A. Cup, and the old city stadium was crammed with supporters. At the end of the game, as thousands of fans exited the arena, Jack and his boy were caught in a crush and for a few terrifying moments, lost sight of each other. Like a large beast, breathing down his neck, the crowd bore down on top of him. It was something the lad would never forget.

Robert sneaked a look over his shoulder. He couldn't see anything, but it was definitely there. He could feel its presence. A dark malevolent spirit, pressed against him, nudging him forward, determined not to let him pause, not even for a second.

And he was struggling. There were stones on the path that he'd never noticed, and as they crumbled beneath his feet, the boy skidded, and then he slipped, straight over the edge.

Immediately gravity assumed control, propelling him head first towards the ground. Robert tried to grab something to stop his fall, but there was nothing to grasp, and as he struggled to claim any of the air that rushed by him, he lunged forward. Two wiry legs flayed around above him. He tried desperately to contort his body into a position where he could see what was beneath him. When all of a sudden, he hit the metal floor with a loud deafening thump.

After everything that Robert and his mother had experienced, all the pain, all the anguish. Their travels through time were finally over. They'd returned to the place from where they started their journey, and sadly, both had suffered the same fate.

Kathy was at Grandpa Gerald's cottage, still battling her injuries. She had severe concussion and a headache that wouldn't go away. Robert was also at Grandpa Gerald's, but evidently not at the house. He'd also suffered a bang to the head. Not as serious as the one his mum had sustained, but he had been unconscious. And for how long… he had no idea. As he dragged himself to his feet, he was struggling to think clearly. The boy was confused, and hadn't got a clue where he was. All along he'd had the notion that he would end up at the castle, but regrettably, he was mistaken.

He was inside a big old cabin, about forty-foot square. And anchored in the far corner, was a metal cage, considerably smaller than the cabin itself. The cage had a steel floor and steel roof. It was about seven foot in height, with steel bars on every side, and each of the bars about five inches apart. There was one narrow door at the front, secured shut with a rusty old lock. It had no plumbing, just a solitary wooden bed on which to rest, and a bucket for slopping out. It was a prison, with one purpose in mind. To contain anyone, who happened to arrive unannounced, from one particular location. And Robert was its only occupant.

And he was still gathering his thoughts when the cabin door opened wide, and as expected, in walked Grandpa Gerald. It was definitely Gerald, although with a huge respirator secured tightly to his face, the boy could have been forgiven for not recognizing the man. The cane, the sun hat and the unmistakable sparkle in Gerald's eyes, was all the evidence that Robert needed.

"Its good to see you up and about." Gerald mumbled. "How are you feeling?"

The boy didn't answer.

"If there's anything you need?" The old man stuttered. "You only have to ask?"

"I want to see my mum." Robert snarled immediately. "And I need to get out of here."

"That won't be possible I'm afraid… not at the moment anyway." Gerald insisted. "Its for your own good."

"Where is she?" The boy growled.

"Don't worry. She's safe." Grandpa Gerald sighed. "She's had a bump on the head, but she'll be okay. I'm looking after her."

"I want to see her." Robert demanded.

"All in good time." The old man nodded. "Kathy needs to rest and recover, but as for you lad… we need to keep you away from everyone, until you've got rid of that infection."

"Infection." The boy screamed. "What the hell are you talking about? What infection?"

"You picked something up in China." Gerald insisted. "I don't know what it is, but it's serious. And until it's burned itself out, you're not going anywhere."

And the truth was, the boy didn't feel well. Some small part of him had known for a while that things weren't right, but he'd suppressed it, unable to admit it, even to himself.

"I don't understand." The boy muttered.

"You've been back almost a week now." Said Gerald. "Most of the time, you've been flat on your back, and it was touch and go for a while. But you are getting better. Although I still can't let you out. Not yet anyway. I need to be absolutely certain, that you're not going to give this thing to anyone else."

The boy coughed.

"You've had some sort of pneumonia." The old man insisted. "And by all accounts, it's very infectious. But if it's any comfort… you're not the first."

"What do you mean?" The boy asked.

"I've been here for many years lad." Gerald explained. "And I've seen lots of people coming and going. And a few of them have arrived from Wuhan, just like you, in exactly the same condition."

"And where are they now?" Robert gasped.

"You don't want to know." Said Grandpa Gerald sternly.

The old man's respirator slipped a little, revealing huge bags below his eyes, much larger and darker than the boy could remember.

"I do want to know." Robert wheezed.

"They're in the ground son." Said Gerald solemnly. "At the back of the garden."

"So what is it?" Asked the boy. "This thing… this infection?"

"I don't know." Said Gerald. "But I hope to God they can find a way to stop it in 2019, because if they don't, it's going to kill a lot of people."

"Is it a new disease?"

"It must be." Gerald bowed his head. "And that's why I can't let you out son. Can you imagine what would happen? There is no cure. There's no vaccine and no medicine. This is post war Britain 1955. The country is on its knees. I'm sorry lad."

The boy nodded.

And then almost immediately, Robert jumped up, total panic etched across his face.

"The book." He screamed. "I found it… and I had it with me… oh please for god's sake… tell me that you've got it?

Grandpa Gerald began to wring his hands nervously. He could hear the desperation in Robert's voice, and see the blood draining from his face. The old man wanted to look away, but he would never do that. He owed it to the boy, to tell him what had happened, to tell him the truth, no matter what, however difficult that might be… What he couldn't do was tell the boy what he wanted to hear.

"Do you have it?" The boy spluttered.

"No… I'm afraid not." Grandpa Gerald sighed. "But we know what you did. And it was everything we asked… I'm so sorry lad."

"But I had it in my hand." Robert insisted. "Before I fell. So it must be here somewhere?"

"Please." Grandpa Gerald begged. "Let me speak."

Robert submerged his head in his hands and slumped down on the bed. He was exhausted.

"Do you remember at the start of the holidays?" Said Gerald curiously. "When you and Kathy went to Skipton?"

The boy grunted.

"Who booked the coach tickets?" The old man asked. "Do you know?"

"Why?" The boy mumbled. "My mum of course."

"No. I'm afraid not." Said Gerald. "It was Jack. He organized everything."

"So?" Robert grunted. "What of it?"

"Jack planned it." Gerald insisted. "He arranged everything… with your Granddad."

"I don't understand?" Said the boy. "That doesn't make sense."

"Your Granddad was in Skipton that day." Said the old man. "He wanted to meet you."

"Well that never happened." Robert stressed. "The first time I met him was in the Lakes, a few days later?"

"Yes I Know." Grandpa Gerald gasped. "Jack had suggested to Kathy that she take you on a cruise along the canal. And that's where your Granddad planned to meet you."

"We didn't do that." Said Robert. "We went to the castle instead."

"I know." Gerald nodded. "And it's a pity. If you'd met him that day, things might have worked out a lot different."

The boy looked up. He was puzzled.

"You weren't his only option." Gerald insisted. "So when he couldn't find you. He made a point of searching out his next victim."

"Where... in Skipton?" Robert gulped.

"Yes in Skipton." The old man agreed. "Your Granddad had travelled through time, and created a new life for himself. And he always looked every bit the gentleman that most people thought he was. But actually, he'd never changed. Not really. Everyone in Ambleside knew him as the local butcher. A war veteran, devoted husband, successful businessman and law-abiding citizen. But in reality, he was none of those things. He was always the same ruthless tyrant that turned up on Vimy Ridge in 1917. He could pretend that he was respectable, but in truth, he never was. And no matter how hard he may have tried to erase the past, he would always be Robert of Rhuddlan. One of the most despised characters that ever walked these shores."

"So. When he couldn't find me, who else did he meet?" Asked the boy.

"His daughter." Gerald argued.

"I didn't know he had a daughter." Robert looked bewildered.

"Yes." Gerald insisted. "And as far as your Granddad was concerned, just another bastard child, and one of hundreds."

"That's odd." Robert snapped.

"I heard him say that, in the castle in 1093. Those exact words."

"There you go then." Said Gerald. "So maybe now, you'll understand what I'm saying."

"But who is she?" The boy was intrigued.

Her name is Maddy." Gerald growled. "She's a chip off the old block. And you've already met her, though I doubt that you two had much in common."

"When?" The boy snarled. "When did I meet her?"

"In Skipton… at the castle." Said Gerald. "From what Kathy has told me…and then again… at Aberlleiniog in 1093."

"The fat girl." Robert roared. "Oh yeah I've met her. She's horrible. So let me guess. Granddad knew all about the tunnel in the churchyard in Skipton didn't he? So he showed her where it was, and told her all about the book? Just like he did with me?"

"That's right." Said Gerald. "He didn't care. He didn't care about you, or her, or anyone, as long as he could get his hands on that book again. That's all that mattered to him."

"So where is she now then?" Asked the boy. "I saw Rhuddlan's men throw her into the tunnel?"

"That's true, but it's unlikely you'll see her again." Gerald sighed. "She was here with me, looking after your Mum. But now she's gone."

"Gone?" Said the boy. "Where's she gone?"

"I don't know, and that's the truth." Said Grandpa Gerald. "And I can't deny, I'm glad to see the back of her. But the problem is, she's taken something that wasn't hers."

Robert's face looked ashen.

"Really?" Said Robert. "So what might that be then?"

Grandpa Gerald couldn't bring himself to spit it out, so the boy helped him out.

"It's Rhuddlan's book isn't it?" Robert screamed. "I knew it... Oh for god's sake. After everything I did to hang on to it. How could you let that happen?"

"I'm sorry son." Gerald sobbed. "I'm really sorry."

"And my Granddad?" Said the boy. "What does he have to say about it?"

"He can't say anything lad." Gerald insisted. "He's   dead."
"What… when?" Cried the boy.

"I got a phone call at the house." Said Gerald. "About an hour or so after you and Kathy had climbed up into the old oak tree and disappeared into the void. It was his wife. She said he'd had chest pains for a few days and that eventually she'd called for an ambulance. But before it arrived, he had a massive heart attack and collapsed. He never recovered."

CHAPTER 20

Saturday, 22nd, October 1955

Chorley town center in the county of Lancashire U.K.

It was almost six months to the day since Kathy and young Robert Rudd had shopped together in town, and during that time, John Bingham the butcher had got even busier. The moment customers stepped inside his shop and shuffled their feet through several inches of fresh sawdust the big man's skills were on display. It was business as usual, and if anything, the slaughterer's handiwork was even more impressive.

But unlike his last visit, Robert stood back and waited for his mum to get served. And contrary to the shin beef that Kathy often bought. She was treating her men to a huge Sunday roast. After they'd travelled back from North Wales and the boy had gone back to school. Kathy had started work again at the pie shop on Eaves Lane, and the Rudd's finances had improved. Jack had worked extra shifts at the Royal Ordnance Factory. And it wouldn't be long before they'd enough money to put down on a new build. Hemmings and Kent a local building firm had started work on a ten-acre plot in the village of Eccleston nearby. What Jack had set his heart on, was a three-bedroom semi with a huge garden. Somewhere his boy could kick a football about, without constant haranguing from the neighbors.

It was half term, and because of that, Kathy had booked a few days off to spend with Robert. He'd struggled at school over the past few weeks, and had problems settling in again. He had a hacking cough, although it was getting better, and his energy levels were low. Kathy was trying hard to feed him up, but the boy was insistent, he had little appetite, and couldn't taste or smell anything. But despite all the difficulties, there was something to look forward to, yet another trip to the Lake District in two days time. Elizabeth Pennington's letter had arrived out of the blue, and the moment Kathy opened it, she smiled. It was the first time she'd smiled for months.

Monday was bright and sunny. It was chilly but not unreasonably cold for the time of year and Chorley railway station was busy with travellers. When the Preston train arrived, there was a bit of a skirmish to get onboard, but nothing compared to the tram stop in Buenos Aires. Robert's memories were still very vivid and often painful, but on the other hand, it was as if he'd never been away.

The train journey from Preston to Oxenholme was quite emotional, reminiscent of their expedition to North Wales a few months earlier. And as they headed off towards the Lakes, aboard yet another monster locomotive, they shunned the city, and what some would describe as the dark satanic mills of the industrial North West. On either side of the track was a level landscape of autumnal shades. And in the distance, further west, much higher ground, where peaks were flushed with color and wrapped in a blanket of fragrant heather. The magnificent fells of the English Lake

District bathed in sunlight and cloaked in their seasonal shades of maroon and magenta.

It was a similar trip to the one they'd taken to Bangor, but under much different circumstances, and with fewer expectations. For Robert, a simple train journey where he could sit back, relax and enjoy the views.

They changed trains again at Oxenholme and climbed aboard a slow train heading north and west, a route through the countryside transporting locals and tourists to the market town of Kendal and ultimately to Windermere, at the end of the line.

Half an hour later Kathy and the boy disembarked at the tiny provincial railway station and hurried across the platform to their waiting bus. And within minutes they were on their way to Ambleside and then subsequently the tiny outpost of Grasmere. A quaint little village at the edge of Rydal Water, where a famous poet called William Wordsworth once described the place as "The loveliest spot that man hath ever found."

Kathy had never been to Rose Cottage, but she had dreamt about it, and then all of a sudden, she was there. And as she strolled up the gravel path with Robert by her side, it was love at first sight.

But before she had time to commit her skinny fingers to the old brass knocker, Elizabeth Pennington opened the door with a big smile on her face and immediately she threw her arms around them.

"Oh it's so good to see you both." The old lady insisted. "I couldn't wait… please come inside. I hope you're hungry."

"Always." Said Kathy.

"And you, young man?" Elizabeth asked. "I bet you're starving aren't you?"

"Oh yeah… definitely." Robert smiled.

"Good." Said Elizabeth. "You sound just like your Granddad."

Rose Cottage was a beautiful detached property, set back away from the road, a magnificent Lakeland house standing in picturesque gardens at the foot of Hellvellyn. Only a few minutes walk from the center of the village in the heart of the National Park. With four bedrooms upstairs and a further two on the ground floor, and every room tastefully decorated. It had a fabulous farmhouse kitchen with a double oven Aga, a large Victorian bathroom, and a sitting room at the rear of the cottage with sensational views of the fells.

And it was there that the three of them sat down for lunch. They had a lot to talk about.

Pennington's widow was stylish and elegant, and always behaved and dressed in a way that people expected of her. She'd played the game far too long to change things now, and despite her recent loss, had no intentions of changing her appearance. She'd incorporated a thick white satin ribbon into her hair, and created a braided bun that she flaunted at the nape of her neck. She wore a chunky white wool sweater, a rust-colored pleated skirt that cascaded out at her ankles, and a pair of flimsy white sandals with delicate diagonal straps.

And she'd been busy. In the middle ground between two extra large sofas was a table crammed with food, with everything from sausage rolls, sandwiches and vol-au-vents and for after's, numerous cakes and pastries. It was a banquet.

"Come on sit down." Elizabeth insisted. "And please… just help yourself. I've been looking forward to this for months."

"It's good of you to invite us." Kathy smiled. "I was so pleased when I got your letter."

"Nonsense." Said Elizabeth. "The truth is, I was desperate to see you. And from what I've learned over the past few weeks… you're family."

Kathy leaned across and touched the widow's hand ever so gently.

"I couldn't have children." Elizabeth sighed. "We did try, but it never happened. Although you probably already know, where I failed miserably… my husband excelled."

Kathy nodded. She didn't know what to say.

"I've spoken to Gerald several times. " Elizabeth urged. "He's told me everything. And I have to admit, a lot of what he had to say has been hard to believe, but I know now that it's true. My husband was a bad man."

"He was very convincing." Said Kathy. "He had me fooled."

"He had everyone fooled." Elizabeth insisted. "And if I'm honest, I always knew he wasn't the man that people thought he was."

"Was he… abusive?"" Kathy whispered.

"No not in the slightest." The old lady stressed. "Not with me he wasn't. In fact… he was just the opposite. I could have anything I wanted. And that's why I never quizzed him. I should have asked more questions?"

"You weren't to know." Said Kathy reassuringly. "You're not to blame for anything."

"All he was interested in was keeping up appearances." Said Elizabeth. "Nothing else mattered. And all along, he was hiding the darkest of secrets."

Kathy squeezed Elizabeth's hand firmly, it was all she could do, that and listen…

"And heaven knows how many women he's had." Elizabeth gasped. "I've lost count."

"You must try to put it all behind you." Kathy insisted. "You've got to move on and start again."

"Exactly." Said Elizabeth confidently. "And that's the main reason I invited you over."

Kathy looked puzzled.

"So Robert… what do you think about the house?" Elizabeth smiled. "Do you like it?"

The boy was trying hard to convince everyone that he was as hungry as Missus Pennington hoped. And with his mouth full of sausage roll, there was a long delay, before he could give her the answer that she wanted.

"Its amazing." Robert said eventually. "It's the loveliest house I've ever seen."

"Good. I'm glad you like it." The widow grinned broadly and turned to face him. "And that's why I decided to see my solicitor last week, and draw up a new will."

Kathy's jaw dropped.

"This house Robert." Elizabeth insisted. "Will be yours one day… I promise."

"Mine?" Whispered the boy. "Why… why me?"

"Because." Elizabeth said. "Because you are the nearest thing that I've got to family. And even though I realize that the man I was married to for all those years, was not the man I thought he was. He never stopped talking about you. He thought the world of you. He had lots of other children and grandchildren, but he never mentioned any of them ever… not once. And that's why I've decided that you, and you alone, will inherit everything when I'm gone."

"But… you have to be sure?" Kathy mumbled in disbelief.

"I'm sure." Elizabeth insisted.

Robert jumped up and threw his arms around the old lady. "Thank you." He cried. "Thank you so much. This is the best day I've ever had."

"Well I'm glad to hear it." Said Elizabeth. "And after what Gerald has told me about your previous adventures, that's a huge achievement."

Kathy joined in with a group hug, tears streaming down her face.

"And Robert… there's something else I want to give you, before you head back." Elizabeth insisted. "Just give me a minute please. And I'll go and get it."

A few minutes later, and the old lady returned with a small wooden box tucked underneath her arm, and between her fingers a tiny key.

Once opened, she slipped her hand inside the box and placed whatever it was she wanted to give the boy, in the palm of her hand. Elizabeth locked the box once more, and placed it on Kathy's lap.

"That's for you Kathy." She insisted. "There's a few things in there I want to give you. Stuff that I've found since Allen died. And if you wish, you can show them to the boy when he's older."

"Of course." Kathy agreed. "I understand."

"Right then." Said the widow as she turned back to face the boy. "So… what do you think? I saw your Granddad gazing at this quite often, although I'd never actually held it in my hand, and never had the chance to study it?"

Robert leaned forward in anticipation. He had absolutely no idea what the old lady was talking about, but still, he was fascinated.

Elizabeth stretched her arm out to its full extent, her fingers tightly shut. And then very slowly she uncurled each one in turn, and exposed the big reveal. It was a five-blade penknife with a wooden handle. A precision cutting tool with several sharp blades, and each one of them made from a high quality stainless steel, nonexistent in the eleventh century. It had however travelled forward in time from 1093 after young Robert Rudd had presented it to the famous Norman adventurer and the Lord of all North Wales, Robert of Rhuddlan.

Robert's Granddad, Allen Pennington had kept the knife under lock and key for the past thirty-eight years, ever since his arrival at Vimy Ridge in April 1917.

"It was your Granddad's prize possession." Elizabeth smiled. "Trust me… he valued your gift more than anything he'd ever owned. You need to look at it closely, he had it engraved."

And sure enough, when Robert studied the knife in more detail, he could see a tiny engraving along its metal spine. In gothic font were four simple words. "Robert The Butcher's Boy."

Tears streamed down the boy's face. He couldn't hold back. It was all a bit too much.

"You know what this means… don't you?" He cried.

"Tell me." Elizabeth insisted.

"When we first met on Lake Windermere." Said Robert. "And Granddad asked me to go back in time, to try and find the book… He knew all along that I was going to do what he asked. It didn't matter what I said to him, or how much I complained. I was always going to obey him. And he knew that all the time."

"And that's why it was easy for me, to make my decision," Said Elizabeth. "You deserve to inherit. It's what your Granddad would have wanted. Trust me. I know."

Back in Lancashire, later that evening, whilst Robert was fast asleep in his bed, Kathy was compelled to take a look in the box that Elizabeth had given her. There were lots of photographs and letters of correspondence, many of which meant absolutely nothing. However there was one particular note that Kathy read several times. It was a letter from a woman called Penny, begging Allen Pennington, to come and visit their daughter. There was a small black and white photograph attached to it, and the face on the photograph was unmistakable. It was a fat girl, about eight years old. And even then, for one so young, the kid looked angry and intimidating. And just like Medusa with a nest of venomous snakes protruding from her head, the fat girl had what appeared to be living braided pigtails that no doubt, whirled around her as she moved. The girl's mother had written her address on the back of the photograph and alongside it, the name Maddy.

Kathy put the letter to one side. She closed the box carefully and turned the key. She pulled the fireguard back away from the fire, and in an instant, threw the box in the center of the blaze, then sat back and watched it burn.

K. E. HEATON

THE END